What the Thunder Said

Tales from the Angels' Share
Volume 2

Marella Sands

Word Posse

Dedication

To all the staff and volunteers at Cahokia Mounds State Historic Site

Acknowledgements

First readers are a blessing! If you produce a manuscript and you don't think it needs improvement, you're wrong. Thanks to Sharon Shinn, Brian Pigg, and Sue Bradford Edwards for their comments.

From Word Posse

Sleeping the Churchyard Sleep, Rett MacPherson
Bad to the Bones, Rett MacPherson
Pandora's Mirror, Marella Sands
Fortune's Daughter, Marella Sands
Restless Bones, Marella Sands
The Water Girl, Deborah Millitello
Do Virgins Taste Better? And Other Strange Tales, Deborah Millitello
Thor McGraw and the Ice Man Murder, Tom Drennan
The Naturalist, Mark Sumner
On Whetsday, Mark Sumner

The Angels' Share Books by Marella Sands
Volume 1: Through a Keyhole, Darkly
Volume 2: What the Thunder Said
Volume 3: The Chair She Sat In

Visit us at www.wordposse.com

This book has been typeset in Fanwood. Cover design by Word Posse. Photos by Golden Mean Photography.

ISBN-13: 978-1-944089-12-2

Praise for *Restless Bones*

"Marella Sands has a keen eye for detail, and an ability to take innocent research and bits of trivia, and turn them into stories that will disturb, frighten, charm, and make you think." Laurell K. Hamilton

"I think Marella Sands may have made a horror short-story fan out of me!" Kaylee Stevens

"Haunting and engrossing, this compilation of tales of spine-tingling horror will have you on the edge of your seat." Brenda Maxwell

"The stories are a great length to read in one sitting—if you can take it! I had goose bumps throughout." Nicole Hastings

"A must read for fans of horror and dark fantasy." Stacy Decker

"I was pleasantly surprised by the top-notch professionalism in this book, from the strength of the narration to the engaging storylines—a real challenge considering the shorter length of these stories. Kudos to Ms. Sands; she will be on my list of authors to watch." Max Gilbert

Praise for *Pandora's Mirror*

"This was a brilliant novel and very well-crafted. I was most impressed with the amazing writing—literary, beautiful, almost poetic prose that made the story even creepier to read." Essie Harmon

"The writing is simply lovely, with literary prose that has powerful, evocative word choices that truly bring this terrifying story to life. A fast read with shocking twists, and a satisfying ending." Nicole Hastings

"Warning—when starting Pandora's Mirror, *make sure you don't have anywhere you need to be or anything you need to do because you won't want to stop reading until you've finished it all!"* Stacy Decker

1

I drank my tea and looked in on my pet hedgehog Petunia. She was rather grumpily retiring for the night. Night, that is, for her, which was morning for me.

The pink and gold dawn was flawed only by the yellow haze which sat heavily on the city of St. Louis and from which we were likely to see no relief in the near future. A high pressure system had parked itself over the area and we were in for a further week or two of high temperatures, high humidity, and no wind. Although I loved cloudless blue skies, the past month of unrelenting record-breaking heat and lack of rain was becoming oppressive.

Petunia yawned and retreated into her box. She was a fairly easy pet to deal with, especially since my live-in boyfriend Castro did the most for her.

He also did almost all of the other chores around the apartment, while I worked to support us. Which I hadn't done for the past several days.

Castro came into the kitchen, whistling some tune I knew I'd heard on the radio recently, but which I couldn't identify. He kissed me before grabbing his morning coffee. "And how's my lovely lady this morning?"

"You mean me or the hedgehog?"

He didn't bat an eye. "The hedgehog, of course. I know how you are: edgy and perpetually pissed."

I almost said something to that, but kept my mouth shut. No mean feat for me. Still, he wasn't wrong. I *was* perpetually pissed these days, and terrified, because I now knew that strange, even supernatural things, were happening all around me, and I wasn't going to have the option to tell them to leave me alone.

That was a tough thing to live with. I hadn't figured out how yet.

Castro looked at himself in the glass front of the microwave and ran a finger through his coffee-dark hair. It was just now long enough to touch the tops of his ears, which meant he was overdue at the salon. "Not looking too good," he said. "I'll get it cut today before I head to the store. Can you think of anything else you want to put on the list?"

I wanted to shout at him that all I wanted was him, and him to be safe. Four nights ago, I'd fought for his life with creatures of ungodly power, and, with help, I'd won. Fortunately for Castro, he didn't remember any of it.

Unfortunately for me, that meant I couldn't talk to him about it, or explain why I was suddenly so very clingy, even to the point of not going in to work. I'd almost lost him. There was no reason another supernatural *thing*—I had no other word to use yet—couldn't come crashing into our lives today and threaten to kill him. What would I do then? How could I handle another attack on Castro?

Instead of saying anything, I threw my arms around him and breathed deeply of his morning shampoo-and-aftershave scent. Lately, I had not been able to get enough of it, and I thought he was likely to lose patience for all this outward display of affection sooner or later. I know he was confused about this sudden desire of mine not to let him out of my sight, but I couldn't help it. I had come too close to watching him die.

"Hey, it's cool," he said. "I'm just going to the store."

I held back tears and looked into his dark brown eyes. "I know. And I can't think of anything to add to the list."

"Movie marathon tonight, or will you be going into work?"

"Marathon," I said. "But something funny." Castro had a tendency to choose movies that bored me. Explosions? Gunfights? Not for me. And his second choice was horror, which normally I didn't mind, but which I had no appetite for now. Considering what I'd met in the underground tomb in Bellefontaine Cemetery four nights ago, I wanted to forget all about ghosts, zombies, demons, and vampires. I had a sinking feeling my life was about to become full of them, or something even more primal, the things on which those legends had been based. I didn't need to watch movies about them, too.

Castro bit his lip in what I considered his "thoughtful" face. We didn't have a ready stock of funny movies to watch; neither did we agree, very often, on what constituted *funny*. But I think he realized that today was a good day to mollify me rather than try to cajole me into watching whatever shoot-'em-up blockbuster we'd missed at the theater and which had just hit Netflix or Redbox.

"So...do you want me to check the store for stuff in the $5 bin, or what?"

I realized I had no idea what I wanted to watch other than I wanted to laugh. I shrugged. "If you see something you think I'll like, fine. But otherwise, we can check for something to stream online later."

"Okay." He looked unsure, but I knew he didn't want to antagonize me.

"You didn't do anything wrong," I said for the hundredth time in the past four days. "I just have some things to work through. About my job. About my boss. About my life."

"I'm part of your life."

"The best part," I said. "That's not what I have to think about. It's everything *else*. Okay, except Petunia. She's not going anywhere, either."

He looked as if he wanted to say something, but thought better of it. He gave me a brief hug and left, still bewildered. But what could I say? I didn't even know what was going on myself.

I stared out the window at the small parking lot behind our building and watched his jeans-and-t-shirt-clad figure emerge from the building and head to his ancient gray Civic. Castro got in the car, pulled out of the space, and headed out onto the street. I watched him until he turned the corner and his car disappeared behind the small Chinese restaurant on the corner.

My heart thumped once, painfully, in my chest I lost sight of the car. *You're crazy, Teryl. He's fine. Let it go.* But I still had a desire to run down the street and turn the corner just to see his car for a few seconds longer. To somehow share a few more moments with him, even if only in a stupid shitty way.

I closed my eyes and leaned against the edge of the counter. I wasn't really crazy, was I? Just afraid of losing him. Afraid of what my boss had meant when he promised to tell me what was going on.

And give me a raise. Don't forget that. He would give me information, and a raise. In response, I hadn't been back to work. I'd just agonized, stupidly, over all the things I needed Castro for, all the things I couldn't bear to lose if he weren't in my life. If he died.

If he were murdered by a monster.

I took a deep breath. *Four days, Teryl. It's been four days. Get off your ass and do something constructive.* If I weren't careful, the very thing I feared would come to pass, and it would be my fault. Castro would leave me because I would become too clingy, too afraid, too secretive. Too *something* that he couldn't deal with or live with.

I couldn't tell him about my dreams, either, and he knew I was having nightmares. For the past two nights, I'd woken him up choking as if I were drowning. In my dreams, I was trapped in a dark place and suffocating. I guess being in an underground crypt fighting for your partner's life will do that to you. I wasn't trapped anymore, but arguing with one's subconscious is a losing proposition.

I glanced around the apartment, wondering if there were anything I could do to push such thoughts aside and to make myself useful. Laundry was out, because Castro was very exacting about how it should be done, and my efforts did not meet his standards. But I could pick up after myself. I put my breakfast dishes in the sink and looked under the sink for the dishwashing soap. I was pretty sure that was where we kept it. If we even had any. Castro often used the dishwasher, but I had no idea how to operate it.

Dishes had to be hand-washed on my watch.

Suddenly, I felt as if I were being watched. Slowly, I stood up straight, for a moment too freaked out to turn around. What if someone were there? What if it were either of the two men who tried to kill Castro, and whose whereabouts were unknown?

They might be here in my apartment. Behind me.

My stomach did a queasy roll and I clenched my fists to stop them from trembling. Slowly, I turned around.

The only thing behind me was Petunia's cage, and behind that, the small front room of our apartment, complete with tattered couch and second- (or third- or fourth-) hand furniture.

The feeling didn't go away, though now it was less focused. Someone was around; they just weren't behind me.

The roof.

The thought popped into my head. It was forceful, as if something wanted my attention and refused to be ignored. That something was on the roof.

Consequently, the roof was the last place I wanted to be. I didn't even know how to get up there. I'd never tried. Why would I? People don't go to rooftops, at least not in any of the buildings I'd ever lived.

But a second thought followed the first, even more forcefully. *Come up or I'm coming down.*

That did it. I couldn't bear the thought of something unholy and monstrous *in my home*. Whatever happened, I had to go to the roof.

A sudden chill made me want to grab a jacket on this ninety-plus degree day but I didn't. The roof. I had no idea what awaited me up there; I only knew I had to go.

I walked as slowly as possible.

2

I climbed the three flights of stairs to the top of the staircase, not even feeling the effort because the dread in my heart was too strong. Finally, I reached the top. The floor of reckoning, as it were.

The door at the top had *No Roof Access* plastered across it. I pushed at it and the door began to swing open. So much for the sign. I suppose it was just to scare kids into going back down the steps. It wouldn't stop a determined person.

Or maybe it was just there to cover the owner's ass should anyone injure themselves up here.

Or maybe the door was usually locked, but whomever wanted me on the roof had arranged for it not to be today. Just for me.

I wished I hadn't thought of it that way.

Hot air blasted me as the door opened widely and I stepped onto the dark roof of the building. This early in the morning, it wasn't nearly as hot as it would get this afternoon, but the asphalt roof had already absorbed quite a bit of the morning heat. Or it hadn't cooled off from yesterday.

That was St. Louis in the late summer.

"Well, I'm here," I said in as firm a voice as I could manage.

"Thought you'd never come," said a familiar voice from behind me.

I turned, surprised to find that my summoner wasn't one of the men who tried to kill Castro, but a friend who'd taken a bullet for me. Who had helped me rescue Castro. Even though it was clear he was one of these same creatures who wanted to harm us. Something that looked human, but was not even remotely of the same family tree.

The bedraggled form on the roof was that of Fish. His auburn hair glinted redly in the early morning sunlight, and his clothes and shoes were just as woebegone as ever.

"You look awfully spry for a guy who took a bullet in the gut four nights ago."

He shrugged. "We heal fast."

I decided not to ask what constituted *we*.

He tried again. "I thought your first question was more likely to be about how I asked you go come up here."

I thought about that. Should that have been the first thing out of my mouth? I had far too many unanswered questions to know the answer to that one, either.

I shook my head. "That's probably the least of it. I thought you were just a barfly, but that's not who you are. Now I don't know what to think."

"Oh, I'm a barfly," he said with forced humor. "Just not a normal one."

Again, I felt as if I were being led to ask something. In this case, I should have said *Normal?* But I couldn't. I was stubborn to the core, and I wasn't about to let Fish get away with this kind of high-drama nonsense.

"I have plenty of questions," I said. "But if I were eager for answers, I would have gone into work and asked Ware." Ware was my boss, the owner of the Angels' Share bar where I worked as a bartender. The one who had promised the raise and information.

Fish nodded. "He'll probably tell you a few things. He ought to, anyway. He's been worried, you know. Because you haven't been back since the other night."

"Do you feel things like worry?"

He gave me a lopsided grin that I used to find attractive in a sort of pathetic way. Fish was always rather pathetic when he was drinking at the bar. What he was now, I had not yet determined. "Teryl, we may not be human, but we have feelings."

"Some of you don't seem to."

He didn't meet my eyes. "They do. They just like to indulge in the negative ones. Greed. Jealousy. Rage."

"Good feelings to have if you're homicidal," I said. "Now, is there a point to this little rooftop reunion, because it's hot up here and I'm not interested in getting heatstroke."

He spread his hands in surrender. "I'm sorry. I thought...well, never mind what I thought. I know Castro probably doesn't remember much, if anything, about that night, so I wanted to wait until he left. But I was sure you'd slam the door in my face if I knocked. So, I just...invited you up here."

"In my head."

He nodded. "In your head. It's not easy, you know, and it only works on a few people."

"But I'm one of these special ones."

He nodded again. "More than you know. It's one reason Ware's half out of his mind with worry for you. He knows how much some of us hate people like you, and how much others want to get control of people like you. How much you'd be hunted if everyone knew about you."

"He said I could go."

"He said *he'd* let you go. He can't say that for anyone else. Hell, I'd let you walk away from all this, too. A lot of us would. But not all."

I closed my eyes and tried my best to stuff fear back down into the bottom of my mind. I was getting better at that, but still not good enough.

"I suspect you'll tell me there are more out there than Marveaux and Garnett," I said, naming the two who had tried to kill Castro.

"Yes."

"And what about Pellagrio? He came by the bar to threaten me, you know." I looked at him; from this angle, I could see the red flecks in his irises, the ones that matched the highlights in his hair. If I looked long enough at Fish, he didn't seem like someone who should bear the name *Fish*. His name should be full of fire. He was a being of conflagration, not water, but what *being of conflagration* really meant, I had no idea.

Pellagrio had, on the other hand, been more a creature of earth. He'd been solid, as if he were immovable unless he wanted to be moved. Yet what movements he did make had been performed with such precision, he'd been almost robotic. I would think that, if he made a promise, or a threat, he'd carry it out no matter what. I could only picture him as being as solid and true to his purpose as a boulder, or a mountain.

Fish shrugged. "I don't doubt he uses his bulk to intimidate people, even some of us that are more retiring and timid. But he likes to keep to himself. He's not predictable, but I don't know that I'd say he's evil. I haven't heard of him doing the things you hear Marveaux accused of."

I left that one alone, too. Let Fish come out and say what he meant, or shut up.

Fish shifted his weight from one foot to another. "I should let Ware do most of the talking, but you haven't come in to work, and something's come up."

"Ware could come here," I said, though I shuddered at the thought. I recalled the last time I'd seen him, in my rear-view mirror, and how I had felt the power coiled within him. Power that I was connected to somehow.

I looked down at my hand, where the marker doodle Ware had drawn on my palm had morphed into a red brand. The red had faded to a dark pink over the past four days, and I assumed it would continue to fade until it became pale or even white. I didn't know what it was exactly, but I did know it tied me to my boss in some esoteric way that was inescapable.

"Yeah, that," said Fish. "Not all of us can do that with our names."

"What do you mean? This says *Ware* in some funky script?"

He gave me the stink eye. I didn't even know Fish could make that face. That gave the day a soupcon of extra weirdness.

"No, no, of course not. Ware's just the name he's using at the moment. That's his real name. In our own script."

One moment of extra weirdness was not enough; it just kept coming. I had had enough. *Our own script.* "And you are...?"

Suddenly, Fish couldn't decide where to put his hands. One hand went in his jeans pocket, the other on his hip. Only a moment later, both arms were crossed over his chest with hands tucked behind his upper arms. He shifted again.

"Just say it, damn it," I shouted. The pigeon on the edge of the roof fluttered off, I presume to find a more peaceful rooftop. "Get it out. You're the one who came here to tell me something, remember? I was staying away."

"Maybe we should get off this roof," he suggested.

Fury rose up in my gut and I raised my right fist to him, the one with the brand. Unexpectedly, Fish jumped backward, hands held out in front of him to ward me off.

"Sorry," he said. His face was lined with worry; every joint seemed stiff with fear. "Sorry, sorry. We are the Forlorn. Some call us the Forgotten."

I didn't lower my fist. The feeling of pleasure it gave me knowing Fish was somehow afraid of this fist was the first pleasure I'd had in days. In the back of my mind, I was pretty sure intimidating Fish was reprehensible. But for now, I was going to go with it and decide if I felt guilty about it later.

"That means nothing to me, and you know it," I said. "Spill. What the hell are *the Forlorn*?"

Fish bit his lip and stepped back to the edge of the roof, frightening off two more pigeons, but I didn't let him think he was safe. I stepped forward. "Tell me now. What is this business about being *the Forlorn*?"

"We're old," he said at last. "Really old. Created long ago. Some people have called us demons. Others called us angels. Others called us gods. We've had all kinds of names, suffered all manner of misfortune and agony over the millennia. We've lost so much of what we used to be."

"So you're some kind of fallen angel?" I couldn't hide the sarcasm. "Pretty wings and harps, and then God gets mad and pitches you out of heaven?"

A tear rolled down Fish's face, but for once, I was not moved to pity or even sympathy. I was in this mess, for better or worse, and so was Castro. Fish needed to come clean.

"No, that's just folklore," he said. "We're the real thing. But yes, we used to have wings." He closed his eyes. "You can't even imagine what it's like, to have wings and to use them to traverse the entire universe." The longing in his voice made me want to turn away in impotent embarrassment, like you would if you caught someone masturbating. The sheer desire for his lost wings made Fish stand up straight, head tilted slightly back, hands at his sides, trembling slightly. As if he could conjure those wings on the strength of his longing alone.

"Mine were the deep red of a coal ember," he said, his voice lower and almost sing-song. He was reliving a memory. "Each feather was tipped in black, and my wings—*oh, my wings!*—they were the most beautiful things in all of creation. And they're gone. Gone forever."

He slumped forward, but his eyes remained closed. I remembered the night he had walked me to my car, and I had seen a scar marring his skin, rising up from under his shirt collar, running from his shoulder onto the base of his neck.

Despite the heat on the roof, my blood ran cold.

Yes, he'd had wings. *They'd been cut off.* I shuddered. Assuming anything Fish said was actually true, who had cut off those beautiful wings that Fish mourned for still? And why?

"I used to fly between the stars," he said, still lost in his own thoughts. "And now, I can barely send a thought to a human without abstaining from alcohol for hours beforehand."

"Wait, you could only send me a thought because you weren't drunk?"

He opened his red-flecked eyes and stared at me. I think he was trying to being intimidating, but it wasn't in him. I understood the color of the highlights in his hair and his irises now. They matched his long-missing wings.

"I drink to dull the edges of what I can sense. To get by. If you could hear the thoughts of humans, you'd be with me in the bar, spending as much time as possible drinking so you could avoid hearing them, too."

I didn't doubt it. I rarely even wanted to hear *my* thoughts, let alone anyone else's.

"You drink to avoid others' thoughts. Got it. And you miss the wings you used to have. Okay. And none of you are using your real names, for whatever reason. Fine. That still doesn't explain why you're here. Today. Putting thoughts in my head to get me on the roof."

"I told you, something's up. You should come to the bar."

I shook my head. "Not going until you tell me what's happened."

"It's Little Girl," he said, naming yet another of these immortal formerly-winged creatures, the one who intimidated the hell out of me. She was well over six feet, dark as ebony, and wore silver bracelets from her wrist to her elbows. I assumed the others called her Little Girl in a poor attempt at humor. She'd told me to call her Babs, but when I'd balked at that, she'd offered the name Oya. It was exotic and seemed to go with her much better than either Little Girl or Babs ever could.

When she wasn't intimidating me, Oya ran mysterious errands for Ware. Errands I didn't know much about, didn't want to know much about, and that I'd spent much of the past four days trying not to think about.

"Yes, so, what's going on with Oya?"

"She's missing."

3

"Missing," I repeated stupidly. "You guys can go missing?"

"We all have enemies," he said. "You met a couple of them and saw them attempt to open a sort of interdimensional portal using Castro's blood to fuel the spell. Let's face it, how many times did you think you'd ever see anything like that in your life outside of some crazy fantasy movie? So why would you balk when I say one of us has gone missing? Or is that simply too mundane?"

He had a point. I had no idea what these people were capable of, who their enemies were, or why I was tied up in all of it.

"Fine. She's missing. Surely that happens every so often if you're really as old as you say. And what could *I* do about it?"

He just looked at me. A sinking feeling nearly swallowed me whole. "Oh. Because I'm one of these special people."

He nodded. "The Lost. You are a human with a special connection with our kind. No one knows how many humans are Lost, but there are always some. Ware seeks them out, tries to keep them close to him, keep them safe. But he's not always able to do that."

Sounded like Fish thought I should throw myself on my boss' mercy. I wasn't sure I was ready to do that. Especially if the best my boss could do was to sometimes keep people safe; after all, *he's not always able to do that.*

The sun popped over the skyline of St. Louis and the direct sunlight made the temperature on the roof soar in an instant.

"I'm getting off this roof. But..." I held up my hand. "You are not invited to my apartment. Not now, not ever. If I decide to go home, you can just stand in the hall. Or better yet, go back to wherever you live."

"If I stood in the hall long enough, Castro would come home and see me there, and you know he'd invite me in," Fish said, entirely too reasonably.

I wanted to strangle him for pointing out how civilized Castro was to everyone, when all I wanted was for Fish to go away.

"Come to the bar," said Fish, wheedling.

"Ware will be angry with you if you don't bring me, is that is?"

Fish hesitated, so I was right. Ware wanted me there, and Fish was the bait to get me to come. Ware had probably said, *tell her enough to intrigue her but not enough to scare her off—just get her here.*

"Something like that," Fish said.

I looked at him sharply.

He shrugged. "I told you I haven't had anything to drink in hours. Your thoughts are going to be fairly easy to read until I've downed at least a fifth of something."

"Great." I took a deep breath. I'd been dreading it for days, but it really was time to confront my boss, either to quit or admit I was sticking around for my own safety. I had to take action, make a decision. Or, in less assertive language, just get it over with.

"Wise choice. Let's go," said Fish.

"You know, that's going to get really old really fast."

"I agree. Why do you think I drink so much?"

I took a deep breath. The jeans and t-shirt I'd put on were just fine to wear to the bar, especially when there'd be no customers.

And my boss wanted to see me because I was special, not because I could dress for an occasion. So I had no reason to go back to apartment aside from grabbing my wallet and keys.

"You're coming?" I asked. "Did you drive?"

"No," he said. "I walked."

Said the man who'd been gutshot four days ago. He was now in good enough shape to hike several miles across town. I just shook my head. No use worrying about how superhuman Fish and the other Forlorn might be. I just had to face Ware and get past whatever information he wanted to lay on me about himself or Oya or whomever might be working against them, or who had me in their sights.

You know, nothing much.

I felt like taking another deep breath, and then another. Somehow, if I just *breathed*, everything would be all right. How stupid. Everything was not all right, and wasn't ever going to be again.

"And don't say anything to that," I muttered as I pulled open the door.

"Didn't cross my mind."

I stopped at the apartment long enough to grab my things. Fish politely didn't even look in, just mumbled something like "meet you at the car" and moved on.

I closed the door and put my back to it, exhausted already by the day. If Fish were right, then I couldn't afford to be ignorant of my situation. I had to have the knowledge I would need to keep myself safe, to keep Castro safe.

On the other hand, I had no desire to know more than I knew now. Bad enough that a kind of fallen angel really existed, and that they thought I was some kind of special snowflake that needed to be eliminated or protected.

How had this become my life?

No point in worrying about it this morning, though, was there? I should go to the bar, talk to Ware, and maybe my options would become clearer.

They couldn't be more opaque than they were right now.

I blew a kiss to Petunia, who was not in evidence, and who, therefore, was probably dutifully sleeping the day away without a hedgehoggy care in the world. I also grabbed a scrap of paper and scribbled *headed to the bar to talk to Ware* so Castro wouldn't worry where I'd gone. Then, with nothing else holding me to the apartment, I grabbed my wallet and keys and left. The sound of the door closing behind me made me shiver, as if it were a death knell. Or at least an omen of something bad.

Or maybe it was just my imagination and I was fucked no matter what. My life had changed and that's the way it was. If I wanted to be safe, if I wanted Castro safe, I'd have to arm myself with any knowledge I could. Even if I didn't want to.

I tried repeating that to myself all the way to the car, but it didn't make the prospect of learning more about the Forlorn and how they would affect my life any more palatable.

Fish slid into the passenger seat as soon as I unlocked the door of my little Escort, affectionately referred to as Nixie. She had taken me everywhere I needed to go for years, and plenty of places I hadn't wanted to go to as well.

"I think Ware could be convinced to order some lunch in," Fish said. "I'm starved. How about you?"

"I ate breakfast twenty minutes ago." Though it seemed like hours.

"Well, maybe food's a bad idea, anyway," said Fish. "But at least there will be alcohol."

If nothing else, getting alcohol in Fish in sufficient quantities to keep him from reading my thoughts was appealing. So there was one reason to get to the bar as quickly as possible.

I was silent on the trip to the Angels' Share, and thankfully, Fish kept his mouth shut, too.

The bar was as dark as usual, but what shocked me when I walked in were the number of people in it. Several I recognized as other friends of Ware's and Oya's. Some I didn't know. But towering over them all, in unconscious majesty, if not in height, was my boss.

Ware wasn't the tallest or most attractive or most well-built man, but he had *presence*. He could hardly walk into the bar without patrons noticing him. I'd seen belligerent drunks suddenly get quiet when he walked by, and a stern look from him had quieted many a potential bar fight.

He was the kind of guy who had enough power that he didn't have to use it. He only had to make you aware that he had it, and that it could be used. Normally, I didn't care about things like that, though it had been helpful the few times he'd come to my assistance with a particularly grabby or rude customer.

I wasn't sure if it was more comforting or alarming that he could probably swat a person like a fly, and hardly notice the effort. The thought might be comforting if he were swatting someone who was threatening me or Castro, but not so much if it actually were me or Castro. And just because Ware thought I was special didn't mean he wouldn't come after me if I angered him.

Who knew that it would take to anger him? I supposed, if I hung around long enough, I'd find out. Not a pleasant thought.

He turned the moment I walked in the bar and crossed the floor toward me, arms out in preparation to give me a hug. I stood there and let him wrap his arms around me briefly. "Teryl, I was so worried," he said softly in my ear.

Despite the fact I had dreaded this meeting, I was heartened to hear that from him.

He dropped his arms and stood back, surveying me critically. His white hair, as usual, laid nicely against his head and his unlined skin made his age impossible to determine. Only his light gray eyes seemed old.

His white eyebrows, tipped in black, now had new meaning for me. I would bet anything his feathers had once been white with black tips.

I shivered. It was impossible to be blasé about having a boss who *used to have wings*.

Who was as old as the universe, maybe. Or maybe not quite that old, but old. Really, really ancient.

"Fish told you a few things," he said, without acknowledging Fish's physical presence in any way.

Fish seemed to consider that a dismissal and sidled off to the bar to grab an entire bottle of Johnnie Walker Green Label. Not going to go for the cheap stuff, I guess. Maybe that had been the agreed-upon payment for getting me here.

"Come, I want you to meet someone," said Ware. He stepped to the side and held out his arm, urging me to walk up to an occupied booth.

One was a woman I recognized as Lucy, a drinking buddy of Ware's. She was normally dressed like an aging hippy—clad in long shapeless clothes that were as ill-fitting as they were boring. She, of course, had a bottle in front of her, but it seemed her drink of choice today was Amrut 100, which put Fish's Johnnie Walker to shame as far as price was concerned. I'd never even tried an Amrut. I wondered if she'd brought her own or if Ware stashed a few in the back: we didn't stock that kind of stuff at the bar.

The other person sitting in the booth was unfamiliar to me. She was small and dainty with cascading sunny curls and intensely blue eyes. Her heart-shaped face was made to smile but her expression was of woe. She looked up at me sadly, and seemed hardly to have the energy to say hello as Ware said, "This is Teryl. She's Lost."

The way Ware said that turned my stomach. I wasn't *one of the Lost*, or *a member of the Lost* or something like that. I was simply *Lost*. The phrasing was unsettling.

"Haven't had enough to drink yet, sweetie," said Fish from the bar. "Shove your thoughts down a bit further, okay?"

I thought *shut up* as hard as I could. Let him choke on it.

"This is Mia," said Ware, indicating the blond woman. "She was the last person to see Oya."

Ware sat down next to Mia, which left me to sit next to Lucy. Fish had told me that was short for Melusine, as if that should mean anything to me, but it didn't.

Lucy merely slid down the booth to sit by the wall. She poured herself another shot of the Amrut and didn't look at me. In fact, she seemed determined to disregard us all, which was odd since she'd been sitting here with Mia before Fish and I walked in. Why sit at a booth with someone you intended to ignore?

Lucy's rather limp dark hair hung in her face, and down her shoulders. Some of it even lay on the table, surrounding her arms and her shot glass. Her eyes remained fixed on her hands.

But she was not whom Ware had brought me over to see. I looked back at Mia. "So, who are you really?"

Mia looked confused. "Who...?"

Ware actually smiled. "She's not one of us. She's Oya's current partner. They share a house near Lafayette Square."

"Oh. Okay," I said. I don't know if Ware expected me to be concerned or insulted by a lesbian relationship, but even if I cared who Oya slept with, why that would make a difference to me when I was sitting in a room with at least three immortal beings was beyond me. On balance, *fallen angels* outweighed *lesbian*. Like, by a million percent.

Mia's face cleared, though it looked no less careworn. "Oh, I see. You thought I was one of *them*." She jerked her chin toward Lucy. "No, I'm just a regular person."

"Are you Lost, too?"

Now it was Mia's turn to stare at her hands, which she had clasped together on the table in front of her. Her nails were painted a delicate pale pink. "No, not even that. I really am just an average, regular person."

"Not so average if Little Girl loves you," said Lucy. Her voice was low and sonorous, like the rumble of the surf. I had never heard her speak before, and I was surprised by how captivating her voice was. I wanted to hear her speak again.

The weirdness wasn't going to stop around these people; I could see that right now.

"Not average at all," said Ware, rather paternalistically, I thought. Whatever the relationship between Mia and Oya, it surely didn't need Ware's approval.

"So tell her what happened," said Lucy. Again, I was struck by her voice. I'd listen to her read a phone book in the same way people listened to CDs of waves breaking upon the shore.

Mia nodded once and appeared to take a moment to gather her thoughts. Then she launched into her story.

"We were going to spend the day at Cahokia Mounds, over in Collinsville. I don't know why she loves that place so much, but she does. We walk the trails there for hours. We had just arrived and had started walking when a sudden storm blew up. Thunder, lightning. It was pretty scary."

We hadn't had any storms lately, so I glanced at Ware. Was this woman on the up-and-up?

He noticed my look. "It was a local phenomenon," he said sourly.

"Very local," said Lucy. I didn't know her well enough to catch the nuances in her voice, but she sounded as annoyed as Ware looked.

None of these people planned to explain anything, clearly. "You're saying Oya did it?"

"No," said Mia quickly. "She can't call storms. She can direct lightning if there's already some in the area, but she can't generate it out of nothing."

That was only half an explanation, but Mia continued right on.

"Oya thought it was funny; in fact, she was gleeful. She told me to head for the car, but when I got there, she wasn't with me. She had the keys, so I couldn't get in the car to wait for her, either. I ran to the museum, but it was closed. So I waited by the doors, under the eaves, until the storm left a few minutes later, and then I searched for her. I finally called Lucy, who came and picked me up. I got our spare key from home and Lucy and Truck brought the car back. Lucy called Ware. That was two days ago. No one's seen her, or heard from her, since."

"You're thinking one of you called up a storm," I said to Ware. After all, as Fish had noted, I had witnessed Marveaux and Garnett doing something crazy that Fish described as attempting to open an interdimensional portal. And Fish was walking around, apparently fully recovered, from a gunshot. *And* he could read my thoughts when he wasn't full of alcohol. *And* none of these people were human, so who knew what they could do?

"Maybe, but *storm* is a strong word. It seemed to be thunder and lightning only, no rain," said Ware. What was he hiding about this storm? I would bet he knew more than he was saying. "But as far as locals go, only Lucy has that kind of power."

"I certainly didn't do it," said Lucy. That explained her presence here, I guess. "Little Girl's an old friend." She placed an odd emphasis on the word *old* that I decided to ignore.

"So, you all have different abilities?" I asked. "Does that mean Fish is the only one who can read minds? And Lucy is the only one that can call storms?"

Lucy and Ware exchanged a glance. Ware shrugged. "Mostly. Fish is the best one at mind-reading that I know of. I can't do it myself. Lucy can do things with water others can't. Little Girl can affect where lightning strikes, at least sometimes. Truck and Yama have their own abilities, but neither of them have anything to do with storms or water." I glanced up at the other occupied booth, now recognizing Ware's other drinking buddies. Truck was a grizzled potbellied guy with a bandana wrapped around his forehead, who looked like he ought to be riding a Harley on the open road. Yama was simply large and looked vaguely Asian. I'd never really gotten a good look at him.

"And what about you?"

Ware gave me a withering look. "We're not here to talk about me today. We want to find Little Girl. I've already tried to find Marveaux and Garnett, but they've vacated the area for now."

I shuddered as he named the two who had threatened Castro's life the other night.

"After Little Girl helped you the other night," he continued, "I thought they might want to take revenge on anyone who was there, but they're lying low. Possibly you hurt them more than we thought. The Lost can be quite powerful on their own, even without our help."

Oh, great. Just what I always wanted: supernatural powers I didn't understand and probably wouldn't want to use if I did.

"And that's why I'm here," I said.

Ware nodded. "We haven't told you what Little Girl is good at yet. But only with the Lost."

I had a really bad feeling about what he was going to say next. When he didn't say it, I blurted out, "Just tell me."

Ware lifted his silver eyes to meet mine. "Possession."

4

I was confused. "Possession? You mean like *The Exorcist* and crap like that?"

Ware actually looked a little embarrassed. "Something like that. What I mean is, Little Girl can inhabit the minds of others, under certain circumstances. Ride them."

"She calls it *riding horses*," Mia said. "I once asked if she would ever do that to me, and she said no. She said not only wasn't I Lost, but that she could never do that to someone she loved."

Ware flinched slightly; he hadn't wanted Mia to say that, and now he thought I'd leave. I was tempted to. God, how I was tempted to run out of the bar right now. Horrified, too. *Possession?* That was way out of bounds, by any measure. I quashed the desire to run and tried prying more information out of Ware instead.

"Let me get this straight. You want me to let Oya...Little Girl...possess me. How is that even possible? You don't know where she is."

"We know where she disappeared from," said Ware. "We can start there. If she's alert enough, she'll be searching for some way to get word out about where she is and who has her."

I shook my head. "How do you know she even wants to be found? For all you know, she's taking a break."

A tiny tear traveled down Mia's face. "Because we've been making plans. Long term plans. She's never said she wanted to go. I think she'd stay long enough to say goodbye, anyway."

"I'm sure she would," said Ware, though I wasn't struck by a vast amount of sincerity. I bet these creatures took off whenever they felt like it, whatever their human lovers thought about it.

"A few of her exes have died recently," said Mia. "Preston had a heart attack at work. Qiana was struck by a hit-and-run driver. We thought those were just flukes. Coincidences. Now I'm not so sure."

I stared at Mia. "So you think there might be someone after Oya's exes, and you're next? Is that why you and I are the lone humans in a bar full of..." I had no good word to use here, because *fucking immortal alien things* wasn't quite something I was willing to say out loud in front of five of them.

Fish said nothing to that extremely loud thought, so either he was ignoring me, or he'd had enough to drink now to get my thoughts out of his head.

"Full of the Forlorn," said Ware slowly. "That's what we usually call ourselves."

"Fine," I said, neglecting to mention Fish had already given me that tidbit of information. "But who else might be in danger of disappearing? Or are Mia and the two she's already mentioned the whole list?"

"There's a few more," said Mia softly. "Helen's in a nursing home, though—Alzheimer's. Babs visits her on occasion but Helen doesn't know her anymore. Besides that, there's Fatima, Dahlia, and Becker."

"You seem to have quite a list of Oya's past relationships," I said. "She actually shared that with you?"

Mia shrugged. "I met a few, like Helen, after I learned the truth about Babs. So I knew she'd have had other lovers, and that some of them would be significantly older than me. She loved them before I was born. Helen's even older than my mother."

"So, did you think that someone might be trying to kill their rivals for Oya's affections? I bet not every break-up was amicable. Or even just mildly unhappy. There must have been some ghastly scenes and fights sometimes."

"I don't know. She didn't tell me the details of her relationships. I never wanted to know, anyway. I figured if she didn't tell me about them, then in the future, she wouldn't be telling things on me, either."

That was one way to look at it. I said, "Fucking lot of good her discretion did any of them, if Oya gave out enough information for someone to locate them."

Ware looked like he was going to say something, but then didn't. I stared back at him. "I suppose you have a string of lovers around town, too, so don't get high and mighty on me."

He said, "We don't know anything. Preston and Qiana's deaths are still likely to be coincidences. We don't know that anyone is coming after Mia, or any of the others."

"We just know someone did something to Oya," I said. "Or do we really know? You haven't really told me why she couldn't have decided to say fuck it and leave."

Ware just looked at his hands.

Mia was openly crying now. "She wouldn't do that. She'd at least say goodbye. I know she won't stay forever: what choice does she have? Does any of them have? They never age, and we do. Eventually, they have to move on."

My phone buzzed. I had a text. I pulled it out and looked to see it; it was from Castro. *Home. Hope bossman nt 2 mad. POK*

That last was Castro's personal abbreviation for *Petunia's okay.* He liked to text me about her whenever he got home. I thought it was endearing. Today, it was an especially heart-wrenching reminder of the familiar and the ordinary life that was rapidly slipping away from me.

I texted back *k.* I wanted to also text *see you soon* but I wasn't sure that was going to be true.

"The plan is for you to go to the last place Little Girl was seen, and if she can contact you, she will," said Ware. "That's all."

That's all, like *possession,* wasn't the essence of everything that was wrong with these people. They could do things like mark our flesh and bind it to theirs, read our minds, and take our bodies. The mere thought of any of it was enough to make a sane person run the other way.

"I'm not on board with this," I said. I wanted to get out of here, but I still didn't know enough to protect myself and Castro. I was trapped until I had more knowledge. At the very least, I could voice my objections.

"But Teryl," said Mia.

Ware waved her silent. "I understand. This is a lot to take in. Would you at least agree to go with Mia to the area where Little Girl disappeared and look around? If nothing else, it will give you two a chance to know each other a little better."

I suppose what he really meant by that was *you might eventually feel so sorry for her, you'll do as I ask.*

Still, as long as I was with a fellow human, in broad daylight, in public, I shouldn't be in danger, right? I'd only have to worry about who or what wanted Oya, and her lovers, to suffer. Assuming that's what had happened.

I could very well be collateral damage.

Not a productive thought, but better me than Castro. "I guess you won't need me for a shift tonight."

Ware rolled his eyes slightly. "You've been AWOL for four days. You think you still have a job here?"

"Yes," I said. "Yes, I do. And a raise. I was promised more money."

Lucy choked. I glanced over and realized she was trying desperately to suppress a laugh. When she noticed me watching her, she turned to me and for the first time I saw her brilliantly green eyes. "You're sassy. I like you," she said. "He's a crusty old man who needs someone to give him some trouble sometimes. Everyone else is afraid of him. You're not."

I didn't know what to say to that. Maybe everyone else was afraid of him for a reason. Maybe I was too stupid to be smart enough to fear him, too.

"So, are we going to Cahokia?" asked Mia. She looked from Ware to me.

"I'm not going with you," said Ware. "I have things here to take care of."

"If I recall correctly, Little Girl's ability to contact the Lost will not necessarily be aided by our presence," said Lucy. "Mia should only be with other humans."

"So you think she'll contact me if she's there? I should walk into this thinking at any moment I'll be possessed?"

Lucy hesitated. "I don't think it's like that." Her hands twitched and she looked like she'd swallowed something vile. She was a terrible liar. I was betting that, even if she'd never experienced it, she'd witnessed this *riding horses* talent of Oya's firsthand. My gut feeling was that she had not liked what she'd seen.

Or maybe she was just a terrible liar and I was reading too much into her body language.

"I don't know what it's like," said Mia, "but if it will help us get Babs back, let's do it."

"You mean *I* do it," I said. "There's no *us* here."

Lucy choked back another laugh. I was starting to hate her.

I looked at Ware. "So, how much am I getting paid now? And what's my job title?"

He appeared to mull it over, though I was sure he'd known exactly what he was going to say days ago. "I'm doubling your base pay," he said. "And you'll continue to work some bartending shifts. But other times, I'll need you to run errands for me. Those may come with...tips."

I didn't even want to know what that meant, exactly.

"In for a penny, in for a pound," said Lucy.

"Can we go?" asked Mia again. "I want to start looking." She looked at me, pleading in her eyes. I broke down.

"Fine. Let's go."

"I'll drive," she said.

"No," I said. "I'll drive. You focus on Oya...Babs. Maybe she can contact you, too, even if you're not Lost. Just tell me where to go." I remembered that Cahokia Mounds was on the east side, in Illinois, but I'd never been there. Just another local who'd never bothered to check out the amenities of my own city.

I slid out of the booth. Ware stood and extended a hand awkwardly to help Mia up. She took it, but didn't seem overly happy about it.

Lucy poured herself another shot of the Amrut and ignored us as we walked away. Fish raised a glass and then turned back to his own bottle.

Immortal sots. Who'd have thought those existed, and that I'd ever work in a bar full of the damned things.

The full heat of the day blasted Mia and me as we exited the bar.

"Holy cow," she said. "That's intense."

Holy cow? Who talks like that?

I showed her where I'd parked Nixie and she got in the passenger seat recently vacated by Fish. Despite the fact this wasn't a large car, Mia looked swallowed up by the front seat. She buckled her seat belt.

"So, what's so special about you?" I asked.

"I told you. I'm not special," she said softly. Mia gave the impression of doing everything softly and gently. In a way, I could see the appeal to Oya. Oya was tall, strong, assertive, and righteously intimidating. You could see her ending up with either someone exactly like her who reminded her of herself, or someone completely her opposite, who complemented her overtly outgoing nature. It made me wonder what her other partners had been like.

I had an excuse to find out. I started the car and drove down the street toward the nearest highway on-ramp. I could make it across the river and into Illinois without help; after that, I'd need some pointers.

"Do you really think these two exes of Oya's that you mentioned were actually targeted? A heart attack and a hit-and-run hardly seem like the work of the same person if so."

"I thought so, too, and then Babs disappeared. Now I'm questioning everything."

"All right. Then what did they have in common, besides being exes of Oya's? Why *them* and not two others? Or you, since you're the one with her now? Did they go to the same gym, or have friends in common, or have the same occupation or something?"

"I don't think they hung out at the same gym," Mia said somewhat primly.

"I didn't mean that quite so literally," I said. "I just mean, is there somewhere that these people may have been seen in the same place? Maybe they didn't even know each other, but they were all Cardinals season ticket holders or something like that. Then maybe someone at the ballpark spotted them and took them out first before going after the people that might take more work to find."

Mia didn't say anything, but maybe she was considering what I'd said. I hoped she didn't come back with *they weren't all season ticket holders*. If she was going to be literal about things, this search could get old fast, and Ware could give up any hope that I'd go along with Mia's crazy plan.

"Preston worked at the stadium," she said at last, and I experienced a stab of despair before she continued. "But I don't know of any connection with Qiana and the Cardinals. Or any other organization. As far as I know, they weren't both members of the zoo or frequent visitors to the Dog Museum or regular bikers on the Katy Trail. I simply don't know what they might have in common besides Babs."

She turned to me, and her impossibly blond curls fluttered with the motion. "But that brings up another thing. You call her *Oya*. I hadn't heard that name before. Why did she give you that name? What does it mean to you?"

Now I wondered what the tiny woman next to me thought I wanted with her lover. Did she suddenly see me moving in on her turf?

"It doesn't mean a thing," I said. "She said to call her Babs, and it just didn't seem to fit her, and then she said to call her Oya. It seems exotic enough to fit someone who intimidates me like she does."

Mia held up her phone. "I just looked it up. Oya is the name of a goddess worshiped in Nigeria."

I didn't know what to say to that. I was still processing the thought that Fish and Ware and their like were angels, or at least the sort of things that had given rise to stories of angels. But gods and goddesses?

I guess it really wasn't all that different. They were supernatural creatures, beyond human understanding. Especially humans living before the Age of Reason, or the Enlightenment, or the Scientific Revolution or whenever.

History had never really been one of my strong suits.

Mia let the statement hang in the air. I maneuvered the car over the Poplar Street Bridge, or the PSB in local parlance. The great shining monument of the Gateway Arch was on our left and ahead of us was the state line.

Finally, I gave in. "She's a goddess?"

Mia shrunk a little. I wouldn't have thought she could get any smaller. "In a way. The goddess these websites reference doesn't really sound like her. Babs likes blue, but Oya's colors are more purples and reds. I've never heard Babs utter a preference for the number nine. I don't think she acts as a sort of gatekeeper for the dead, welcoming them to their new life on the other side."

I thought of the wriggling thing that Oya had carried in a sack four nights ago, and how I was pretty damn sure it had been a physical manifestation of a human soul, but I kept my mouth shut.

I had no idea what she had been doing with that soul, but welcoming it to the next world would not be my first guess. Especially since she had sacrificed it without any obvious qualms.

"So she's not the same as the Oya from Nigeria," I said.

"It's not that simple. I think sometimes people encounter the Forlorn and sort of...adapt some aspects of them to their local beliefs. Like, maybe some village worships a sea goddess with certain attributes but then people see Lucy do something magical with water, and the sea goddess then gets green eyes and long hair. Something like that."

"They add to the story rather than being the origin of it."

"Maybe. Sometimes. Who knows? They've been around a long time and Babs doesn't usually tell me a lot. She drops hints or references things and I have to fill in the blanks. Like, once, when I overheard Lucy talking with Babs, Babs teased Lucy about swimming in the Boyne. I don't think either realized I'd heard them. I looked it up later, and there's a river goddess who supposedly created the River Boyne in Ireland and drowned in the resulting flood. But is that what Babs was referring to? I couldn't tell you for sure."

"Is it important?" As the countryside of Illinois flashed by, I thought of something else. "And where are we going?"

"At the split, take I-70, not I-64. I'm not sure of the exit number but there's a sign about Cahokia Mounds. It's brown."

"Okay."

She was silent for a while. I figured she'd forgotten my other question or didn't want to answer it. I concentrated on the signs at the road's edge and looked for one that was brown rather than green.

"I'm not sure it's important," she said at last, very softly. "I just love her so much, and I know she'll never share herself entirely with me."

That was definitely a conversation-ender. I said nothing and simply looked for the road sign.

It wasn't far. I got off the highway and followed the signs to the mounds. I figured the place would be a national monument or something but the signs clearly said *State Historic Site*.

"This is one of Little Girl's favorite places?" I could hardly credit it. The site's grass was a bit brown from the extended hot and dry summer we'd had, but mostly the place looked like some random low hills with one massive hill to the left of the road. The large hill had stairs going up to the top. Several people were hauling themselves up the shadeless path even now, in the heat of the day.

People are crazy.

"Yes," said Mia. She looked relieved to be here. Possibly she was relieved to get out of the conversation we were having. I would be, if I were her. "She likes to walk the trails, and she gets this faraway look on her face when she scans the plaza, like she's remembering how it used to be."

"You think she was a goddess, or whatever, here, too?"

Mia shrugged. "Maybe. Or maybe she just visited. She's never said."

I pulled into the Visitor's Center driveway and headed for a parking space. The lot was nearly full, which meant only spots directly in the sun were left. Nixie was going to be an oven by the time we got back.

That was St. Louis in the summer. And summer in St. Louis could stretch well into October some years. This was promising to be one of those years.

We got out of the car. I expected Mia to head for the Visitor's Center, but instead, she headed to the left of the building, through the parking lot.

"Where are we going?"

"To the last place I saw Babs."

I looked longingly at the building, which promised air conditioning, but followed Mia through the shimmering heat-filled air. Sweat trickled down my face and back. I was going to need three showers to get rid of this day at the rate we were going.

At least when we reached the sidewalk that led west toward some tall mounds, we had a few shade trees to help protect us from the weight of the summer sunlight. It wasn't much, because the humidity was out of sight, but at least it was something.

Despite being at least half a foot shorter than me, Mia walked quickly and I had to focus to keep up with her. She obviously had a destination in mind and wasn't going to let anything distract her.

Her hurried gait reminded me of Castro. He always seemed to be determined to get somewhere a full minute before I did. I don't know why. He just shrugged and tried to remember to walk more slowly, but after a while, he'd forget and start speeding ahead again. That habit was one of the few things I found to get annoyed about on a regular basis.

All in all, it wasn't a big thing, considering he'd nearly died a few days ago. My heart squeezed against my ribcage painfully for a brief moment. I wondered if Castro were home yet, and had seen my note. I wanted to text him to see if he were ok.

I wanted to just have him here with me.

I pushed those thoughts aside. I was more than capable of spending a few hours away from Castro, even after what had happened the other day. I'd see him again this evening.

The sense of dislocation, of something being wrong in my life that I couldn't just fix, was disquieting and, on top of the heat, made me feel slightly dizzy. This must be how Mia was feeling, only since Oya was actually missing and not just at the grocery store, she had to be feeling a thousand times worse.

Maybe Ware's plan to make me feel sympathy for her was working. Damn him.

Mia had plunged on ahead, and we had left the Visitor's Center behind. We walked past a house incongruously sitting in between the center and two large mounds. The sidewalk suddenly narrowed; I supposed the part we had been on doubled as a driveway for whomever lived in the house. The oddity of the structure was puzzling, but I had no time to contemplate it because Mia continued her relentless quest for a particular location.

Just past the house, she took off into the grass to the left of the sidewalk, cutting off a corner of the concrete path.

"Should we be on the grass?" I asked.

"Just don't climb the mounds."

Okay. I followed her through the grass, hoping no ticks or chiggers were in the vicinity, and wondered where Mia was headed. The path went about another hundred yards and passed a much smaller mound to the left. A large interpretive sign stood near a bench. Mia stopped and looked around.

"This is it."

"This is where you were? What's here?" The concrete ended and the path continued on as gravel and bare dirt. Twenty or so yards ahead of us, it entered the woods. In the distance, I noticed a deer walk off the trail. I didn't think they came out in the middle of day.

"This is the spot Babs always comes to first," said Mia with determination. She glanced around. "There must be something important to her here. I always thought it was the view of the Twin Mounds," here she gestured toward the two large mounds we had passed on our way. "But maybe there's something more."

I glanced at the interpretive sign, which declared this to be Mound 72. It showed a diagram with a lot of skeletons. The tiny mound in front of us had apparently been used as a last resting place for a lot of people. Castro would have been fascinated by it.

I read some of the text. "Four male skeletons had their heads and hands missing, and their arms linked together? What's up with that?"

"No one knows," said Mia. "Babs never seemed that interested in the mound itself, though. She'd come here and stop to take a look around, but she never seemed to focus on one thing over another."

A strange feeling made me glance up. Something...odd...was nearby. It took me several long seconds of staring to spot it in the branches of a large tree. What could be that large? It was too big to be a bird.

I remembered a news story about how a mountain lion had managed to capture its own image on a trail camera just a couple counties north of here. So it wasn't impossible for it to be a very big cat, just improbable. Bears were found in some counties in Missouri, but I'd never heard of one in Illinois. Again, just barely possible, but very improbable. Chances were, this wasn't a bear or a mountain lion. Yet there was *something* in the tree. Time to leave.

"Something's here," I said softly. "We should go back."

"We're alone, except for a few hikers stupid enough to be out in the heat," said Mia. She sounded distracted and worried. "What could be so important about this spot to her?"

"No, there's something watching us. Let's go." I couldn't explain the odd feeling, but I knew I was right. The object was very still, but that didn't matter. I could sense its presence.

Mia rounded on me, hands on hips. She was so dainty, she looked like a pouting child. "Teryl, I know you don't want to be here, but..."

Whatever was in the tree decided it had waited long enough. A black shape leaped from the branch where it had been resting and plummeted the twenty or so feet between it and the ground.

It was a man. He landed lightly and stood as if he took jumps like that every day.

My heart leaped in my throat and I swallowed heavily. I shoved Mia behind me and wondered if anyone were close enough to hear me if I screamed for help. Despite the heat, I shivered at the figure under the tree as he regarded us.

The man, who was well over six feet, was dressed in black and wore a long-sleeved hoodie, which seemed insane in this weather. Black pants and boots completed his one-note ensemble. I knew I'd seen an outfit like that before, and fairly recently. The man shook his head and pushed the hood back. His dirty white, almost beige hair was streaked with dark brown and his skin was extremely pale.

Pellagrio.

He had come to the bar last week, to drink whiskey and do his best to intimidate me. In that, he had been successful. Ware had thrown him out of the bar for reaching his large hands toward my throat. And for calling me a bitch.

"Stay behind me," I said as evenly as I could, though my voice shook.

Pellagrio stopped about ten feet away on the grass. "Good afternoon," he said in his clipped voice. He glanced at Mia. "You have a new friend, I see. You working at the bar now, too?"

"Who are you?" demanded Mia. "You know Babs?"

"Babs?" He cocked his head as if trying to recall someone with that name. After a few moments, he nodded. "Oh, yes, *Babs*. I've known the Sapphire at the Eye of the Storm longer than your world has existed, missy," he said with a kind of bored derision.

I almost asked "the *what?*" but didn't really want to engage Pellagrio in a conversation.

"Oh," said Mia with derision in her own voice. "And who are *you?* The Poorly Dressed in the Field of the Sun?"

I gritted my teeth. Antagonizing Pellagrio was hardly a great plan.

"Perhaps we should just go," I said. I tried backing up, but Mia wasn't having any of it. I bumped in to her, and she did not move. So much for pushing her back up the trail behind me.

"No," she said. "I'm not going to be chased off by one of *them.*"

"*They* seem to have some pretty impressive abilities," I said without taking my eyes off the man in front of me. When he was not deliberately moving, like walking or gesturing with a hand, he was absolutely still. Just as he had been in the tree, and last week in the bar. As if he were some kind of simulacrum of a human who only moved when absolutely necessary and was otherwise inert. "I suspect we will be chased off whether we wish to be or not."

Pellagrio actually laughed at that. "You're right there, bartender. But you gave out decent whiskey last week, so maybe I won't chase you off just yet. I'm curious as to why you're out here with the Sapphire's latest plaything, anyway. Why would Ware send you out here with someone else's pet?"

"I'm no one's *pet,*" said Mia. She stepped around me. I put up my arm, but she knocked it aside and strode forward. This woman clearly had *no* survival instincts.

The best thing for me would be to leave. Mia was determined to stay, after all. I should go and let her do whatever it was she intended to do against an opponent over twice her size.

But I couldn't. At the end of the day, you had to look at yourself in the mirror, and I couldn't do that if I walked away from Mia and left her with Pellagrio. Even Ware had said to be careful of the man, that he was dangerous.

If Ware thought someone was dangerous, then he was, because Ware certainly was.

"Pellagrio, just leave us alone," I said, hoping to forestall any action on his part.

But it was no use. He stared at Mia like a hawk stared at a mouse, and stepped forward. Mia ignored the looming danger and looked up at him with defiance. As Pellagrio took a second step, fear pushed me forward and I ran toward Pellagrio, yelled "leave her alone!" and struck out with my right hand.

An electric shock shot up my arm as my palm contacted his face. My arm was thrown back by the force of the blow, and Pellagrio was knocked several feet backward and fell, landing on his ass on the sidewalk.

Both he and Mia stared at me with identical looks of astonishment. "Who the hell taught you to do that?" Pellagrio demanded from the ground. He got his feet under him slowly and got up, but with much less swagger than he had shown just seconds earlier.

"No one taught me anything," I said through clenched teeth. My arm ached and my spine tingled in a most unpleasant way. Even my teeth felt rattled in my head.

Pellagrio glanced at my hand and his attitude remained cocky, but much less aggressive. "It seems Ware's claimed you for his own."

"That's what Ware thinks," I said. "That's not to say I've chosen him."

"Not sure you'll get a choice on that," he said. He actually sounded somewhat sad.

I did not want to start feeling positively toward a man who'd done his best to intimidate me in the two times we'd met.

"Are you willing to leave us alone now?" I asked. "We're here to look for Oya, not deal with you."

"The Sapphire's missing?" he asked. "I'd heard the rumors, but I don't believe everything I hear. And you're here because..."

"Because Babs is missing, and Teryl is Lost. We're hoping Babs can reach out to her mind."

Pellagrio appeared to consider that a moment. "The Sapphire's no telepath. You mean..." he looked at me.

"Yeah. Possession. But screw what *she* says. I'm here to help her look for Oya, not get possessed. When she said *we're hoping* she means *she's* hoping."

"Why won't you help?" Mia demanded, rounding on me. Her voice was shaking and her eyes leaked tears down her pink cheeks. "And why won't you use her name? She's Babs."

Before I could say anything, Pellagrio spoke up.

"She is to you, sweetie," he said. "Not to me. And, apparently, not to the Lost here. Besides, if you know about us, you know we've used many names over the centuries. *Babs* is actually one I'd only heard once, a long time ago, which is why it didn't register right away. It doesn't suit her."

That was one thing he and I agreed on, but I wasn't about to say so out loud.

"So what is it *you* can do, and can you help us, or not?" Mia said. "Otherwise, go away."

Pellagrio's eyebrows shot up. "Bossy little thing, aren't you?" I can see why the Sapphire likes you. She doesn't go for the shy, retiring types."

Mia shrank a little at that, belying the comment. But perhaps she was distracted by thoughts of her lover lost or trapped or...

"Can you die?" I asked.

Mia squeaked, "What?"

Pellagrio laughed.

"Why would I tell you?"

"Because I want to know if I'm wasting my time. Could someone have killed Oya and then made sure no one knew about it? Could *you* have killed her?'

Pellagrio's face became a mask and he stared at me for so long, my heart pounded. I was absolutely certain he was about to pounce on me and rend me to pieces. But I couldn't move. I could just stare at him, my amber eyes fixated on his dark brown ones. The world around us stilled as well; even the cicadas stopped their incessant racket.

Finally, he relaxed slightly. "I think you'd have to be pretty stupid to ask me that seriously, and I don't think you're stupid. Ignorant of us and our history, sure. Stupid, no. So I'll answer your question."

I let my breath out in a rush. I hadn't even been aware I'd been holding it. My knees felt wobbly, but at least I'd stared down one of the most daunting figures I'd ever met, and lived to tell about it.

Sometimes, I could be really stupid, just not in the way Pellagrio had meant it.

"No, I didn't kill her," he said to the renewed singing of the cicadas. "Yes, we can die. But, as far as I know, it's only happened once. And the consequences were pretty dire. Not comets-that-wipe-out-the-dinosaurs dire, but fire-and-plague-gut-London dire. If Little Girl were dead, we'd be hearing about earthquakes or storms or the river running with blood or something. So she's not dead."

"It only happened once?" I asked. "Who was that? What happened?"

"I wasn't there, and I've answered your question."

He blew us an air kiss and walked into the woods without making a sound.

"Who is that guy? You know him?" asked Mia.

"I only know the name he gave me: Pellagrio. Ware said he could be trouble."

Mia looked resolutely back toward the tall mounds that stood between us and the Visitor's Center. "Well, trouble or not, I don't necessarily believe him. I bet they can die easier than he says, but I hope he's right that no one's killed Babs." She wavered on her feet and clutched a locket she wore around her neck.

"We should get in the air conditioning," I said. "The heat's horrendous."

This time, Mia acquiesced. "All right. Babs wouldn't want me to hurt myself while I looked for her. Are you sure you don't feel anything?"

"I don't even know what you mean by that. What am I supposed to be feeling?"

Mia shrugged helplessly. "How do I know? I'm not Lost."

"Well, how do *I* know? I didn't even find out these people were eternally drunk immortal beings until this morning."

Mia remained steadfastly literal. "I don't think all of them drink like Lucy. Babs doesn't usually."

I did my best not to roll my eyes.

A wisp of smoke drew my attention. Where Pellagrio had stood, a small black patch showed in the grass. I hadn't noticed Pellagrio holding a lit cigarette, but maybe another visitor had tossed down a butt at some point today and it was still smoldering. Stupid people should know not to throw away burning items in the middle of a heat wave when everything was dried out and ready to go up in flames with only slight encouragement. Not that throwing away items that were on fire was ever a good idea.

I stomped on the spot and, after a few moments, it stopped smoking.

We headed back toward the Visitor's Center. I couldn't wait to get inside. The dark, oppressive feeling of my dreams was coming back, and it was lodging behind my eyes like the promise of a major headache. Dehydration was a bitch. My limbs felt like boiled noodles.

Actually, I just felt rather weak and sick all over. Air conditioning never sounded so good.

5

The Visitor Center was a pleasant place, with tall ceilings and a large diorama of the site right in the main lobby. It was not, however, particularly cool.

Still, it was cooler than outside. Mia and I sank weakly into chairs at a table in an area marked Cahokia Café, which only lived up to its name if you stretched the term "café" to mean a place where you bought your snacks and drinks from vending machines.

Mia looked wilted, and I hoped rather meanly that she looked more wilted than me. Even her curls sagged, and her cheeks were turning a brighter shade of pink than they'd been all morning. I didn't know if that was sunburn or heatstroke, but I figured I'd better get some water in her. In both of us. I rooted in my pockets for change and found enough to get each of us a bottle of water.

"Thanks," she said. "The heat's brutal." She clasped her locket again.

"I assume that's something Oya gave you," I said. "You seem to treasure it."

She looked confused for a moment, then realized what she was doing. "No," she said. "Actually, this was from my dad. He gave it to me on my sixteenth birthday. He died a few days later. Cancer, you know. My mom hung around until I graduated from high school, then took off with a boyfriend. She called me once, from Jamaica or the Dominican Republic, or something. Drunk, and wanting to let me know how great it was to lie on the beach next to a hot guy. She didn't say whether or not the hot guy was the same one she'd taken off with, or if she'd traded him in for another. I didn't want to know."

She sipped her water and stared ahead sightlessly. I had a feeling I did not want to know what she was thinking about if it was family-related. I took a swig of my own water and scanned the part of the lobby I could see from the table. Perhaps twelve to fifteen people were sauntering through, some of them small children.

Mia heard the children giggling and her face changed. She looked around longingly.

Living with Oya would present a problem if you wanted children, though I guess there were ways around that. Except that made me wonder how much scrutiny Oya's life would take from an adoption agency. Or any other agency or person, for that matter. How *did* the Forlorn change their names and addresses and occupations and continue to exist in the world where everyone was rapidly becoming a number? On television and in the movies, people simply swiped the identification of a dead person. Could that really work?

Well, it was none of my concern, anyway. If Mia wanted kids, she was going to have to figure out how to cope with an immortal lover and her desire to reproduce.

"So, if you just discovered the truth about the Forlorn today, I guess you're not involved with one of them," said Mia in an apparent bid to change the subject.

"No. I live with a guy. Castro. We have pet hedgehog."

I'm not sure why I included the detail about Petunia, except maybe it seemed like something that would put Mia in a better frame of mind. Cute animals can do that, at least if you're Castro or me.

"What does Castro know? About you. About Ware? About Babs?"

"Nothing. Hell, Mia, what do *I* know?"

She shrugged. "At some point, you'll have to tell him. He'll be in more danger if he's ignorant of what's going on in your life. That's one reason Babs tries to limit her lovers to people who don't have families. That's not true of all her lovers, but she prefers not to face those kind of entanglements; she'd rather a broken heart and let someone go than see their family get drawn into whatever conflicts are going on in her life."

I bit my tongue to keep from saying *he's already been in danger and I didn't even know why!* She was probably right. Castro had nearly died when I didn't know anything, and he'd had no way to know to be careful. If he and I were going to stay together, he'd have to know.

If we stayed together? Why wouldn't I stay with Castro? We got along great, he was sexy and liked to cook, and he even liked to take care of Petunia. Maybe it was Mia's talk of Oya trying to limit her partners to a certain kind of person that had me thinking melancholy thoughts about my own relationship. I had no plans to let Castro go.

"He's a nice guy, I guess," she said. It wasn't quite a question, but it was clear she was angling for a bit more information.

"Sure," I said. "He's the best. Does the laundry, takes care of Petunia, cooks. He's gorgeous and great in bed. What else do you need to know?"

That came out a bit more sharp than I'd wanted, and Mia flinched.

"Sorry," I said. "It's just that he was almost killed the other night. I'm still kind of raw."

She nodded. "That's at least one worry I don't have. Even if Pellagrio's telling the truth, and one of the Forlorn *did* die, it was only once, and a long time ago. Babs shouldn't be in any danger, not real mortal danger like your boyfriend was in, anyway. But I'm still worried."

Mia drank some more of her water. She didn't look nearly as peaked anymore.

"You're looking better," I said, in my own bid to change the subject.

She pushed a lock of hair back behind her ear. "I feel better. I think I'll be able to keep looking for Babs, if I just take another few minutes off my feet."

"Well, we have a few minutes," I said, though privately thought neither of us needed to go back out in the sun today.

Mia smiled sadly. "You know, the first time I saw her, I thought *who is this goddess?* I just wanted to be near her so badly. And when she smiled at me, it was like sunlight pouring in a window. I *basked* in it. I guess it's different for you, being Lost."

"How so?"

"The Lost are special. I don't know if you are all the same, but some of them have enough power of their own to be dangerous to the Forlorn. Lucy told me the story of one of her lovers from, oh, the twelfth century—I don't know, a long time ago, anyway—and he could manipulate the Forlorn without them being aware of it. She saw him do it with others, but then he did it with her. He wanted to be a king or something and wanted her help to get on the throne. When she said no, he started working on her. He used some power on her and she helped him get what he wanted, even though she didn't want to. When she realized what he had done, she killed him."

"Oh." Note to self: don't piss off Lucy.

"I think it's one of the reasons she's still so withdrawn today," said my companion. "She remembers that betrayal and it colors everything in her world, even centuries later."

Ugh. I didn't really want to know about Lucy's dead exes, especially when she'd murdered them. But the story had a much more cogent point than that: I might have some power against these creatures. That sounded promising, though clearly working against someone like Oya or Ware would be dangerous.

I glanced at my right palm. Ware's mark was branded on my hand, whether I liked it or not. He'd said he meant it for protection, but it bound us together in ways I couldn't understand. I'd bet it meant I couldn't operate against Ware, in any case. Or, if I'd tried, he would probably know somehow. But thinking I could possibly find some way to oppose homicidal assholes like Marveaux piqued my interest. I didn't want to be a pawn in his games again. I didn't want to have him holding Castro's life over me a second time. Once was more than enough.

Mia saw the direction of my gaze. "Babs mentioned that some of them can make that mark, but I don't know what it means. I'm not sure the Forlorn can mark humans like that. Ordinary ones like me, I mean. It might be just for the Lost. When she told me about it, it sounded like, when she saw that, she finally realized how serious Ware was about getting you on his side."

"Huh." I remembered the other night when Oya hadn't seemed that interested in what I was doing until she'd seen my hand. Then suddenly she'd been extraordinarily helpful, for no reason I could see at the time. "I don't know if I have a side right now. Or if it's the same one Ware is on."

Mia contemplated that for a few moments.

"I've only met him a couple of times, and I found him frightening," she said. "But I can't recall anytime Babs has said something about him deliberately harming the people he wants to protect. If he said he'd let you go, even though he really wants you to stay, he'd probably do it."

"Of course, that may just mean he knows the others won't really let me go," I said.

"Probably," said Mia in a tiny voice. "But as one of the Lost, you likely weren't getting away in any case."

I put that aside. I couldn't deal with that right now. I still wanted to sleep through the night without feeling I was being dragged down through the earth and was choking on clods of dirt. How could I accept that I'd never have been able to avoid that, no matter what?

I knew I'd have to ask Ware what it meant to be Lost. What it *really* meant. If the Lost were just ordinary people who could operate against the Forlorn, why didn't they just kill us once they'd identified who we were? Why bother to try to get us on anyone's side?

But then, how did I even know there really were such things as the Lost? Maybe we were just the ordinary people simple enough to be duped by a *you're special like no one else!* scam.

"But what do they want? What do they do? Besides drink. I mean, Fish comes in *every night*. He's not one of Ware's drinking buddies but I always knew they had some kind of history. Now it sounds like they have an eternity of history. So what's Fish's story? Marveaux's? Ware's? Do they just sit around and do nothing, or do they have plans beyond one-upmanship? Or what?"

"You'll have to ask them. I don't even know most of Babs' story. Just what she wants to tell. It can be hard to get her to open up about anything."

"You'd think they'd want to rule the world, or set themselves up some kind of magical kingdom. Enslave humankind, something like that. Instead, they own bars, drink in bars, and jump out of trees at people. It doesn't make any sense," I said with disgust. How could I figure any of this out?

"You can't look at it like that," said Mia. "You're looking with your head. You should look with your heart."

"Like you and Oya?"

She shrugged and finished her water.

"Why do you stay, now that you know your lover will never age or be someone you can share a life with?" I thought of her expression when watching the children. I'd never contemplated having them; I was sure I'd be as miserable a parent as my mother had been. But Mia clearly thought differently. Loving Oya must put a big complication in her life.

She sighed. "Why does anyone stay with the person they love? Somehow, they complete you. You wake up in the morning, knowing they'll be there. That theirs is the first face you'll see. You know what makes them laugh, and you love to hear them singing in the shower. Without them, your heart is smaller somehow, but with them, it expands to include the whole world. She is my everything, even though I know one day she'll find someone else. But really, what choice does she have? I have one life; she has an eternity. Unless she wants to be alone, she has to move on. Like a shark, never stopping, never resting. Only happy for a few short years before realizing it's been too long, you have to find someone else."

"A lot of people wouldn't understand," I said. "They'd be angry."

"I'm not angry," said Mia. "I pity her. I pity them all. And I pity everyone they accept into their circle as friends or lovers, especially those poor souls they fall in love with. Them especially."

There wasn't a thing to say to that. We finished our water in silence. From outside came a distant rumble of thunder.

6

After a few more minutes, I was more than ready to leave. At first, I thought I just wanted to go home, but home was to the west. For some reason, I really wanted to go south.

"Mia, is there something south of here that's special to Oya?"

"Not that I know of," she said absently. Her attention had been snared by another small child.

I glanced out the window toward the flat area behind the building. To the left were the two mounds we'd already walked past. Ahead was the flat area—the plaza, as some sign we'd seen had informed us—and to the right of that was the road. Across the road was the hulking form of Monk's Mound, a 100-foot tall pile of dirt that had supported the main buildings that housed the leaders of Cahokian society.

Something bothered me about the vista out the window. Something was wrong. Very wrong. I blinked and tried to figure out what it was. The grass was dry, sure, but everything was during this heat wave. Few people were out, which was not surprising, given the ambient temperature of the day.

Still. I couldn't help the feeling that something was very wrong. I got up.

"Teryl?" asked Mia.

Her voice seemed a million miles away. I headed toward the exit and walked out onto the patio. The heat hit me in the face but that was merely a distraction from the gleaming sight in front of me. The plaza flickered as if two pictures had been superimposed, like one of those Halloween decorations that was a normal picture from one angle, and showed a zombie or ghoul from another.

I blinked a few times. In front of me was the grassy area of Cahokia Mounds State Historic Site. But it was also the bare dirt of an ancient city. All around me were dark-skinned people with black hair, moving along well-defined paths. Small dogs nipped at their heels.

Ahead, in the plaza, stood multiple small ramadas. Underneath each one sat several people, who reached out to people passing by while gesturing toward the mats or pots or tools in front of them.

The haze and acrid smell of thousands of hearthfires surrounded me. I walked forward until I bumped into something. The people around me took no notice.

Teryl Teryl Teryl said a voice. Someone shook my shoulder.

I blinked and the plaza was sere and empty of people once again. I looked over. Mia stood next to me, worry in her delicate features.

"Are you all right?"

I glanced around. No one was about. What had I seen?

In front of me was a low brick wall. That was what had stopped me from walking farther into the plaza. I hadn't really been someone else, I had just hallucinated it.

Was I all right? I had no idea what had just happened. I'd never hallucinated before. Was it the heat? An overactive imagination now that supernatural occurrences were upsetting my life?

"Teryl? Are you all right?"

I wiped my sweaty brow with one hand. "I don't know. I feel...strange."

"You looked like Babs looks when she comes here. Like she's remembering something."

I shook my head. "She might remember this place. But you know there's no way I could."

She patted me on the arm. "I bet it's the heat. And it's past lunch time. Let's get some food."

"Well, not here," I said as brightly as I could. "The Cahokia Café isn't quite equipped."

"No, I suppose it isn't," Mia said. Her good humor also sounded forced.

"So where should we have lunch?" I asked.

Mia hesitated. "Well, there's a pizza place in Belleville, near Our Lady of the Snows."

"And we should go there because...?"

"Well, for pizza, for one thing," said Mia with some asperity. "I'm starved. It's been ages since breakfast. And also, Jordan's there. He's...he's someone who's important to me and Babs. He's actually one of her exes." Mia seemed to have to difficulty saying that. *One of her exes.* "If someone is targeting us, we should see if he's okay, or if he's noticed anything unusual. He was with Babs before he was deployed overseas. While he was gone, she met me. So if someone's after her, he might be the one to ask, since he's had more recent knowledge of who she talked or where she went than someone like Helen, who hasn't been in her life for decades."

"You mean we should ask him if Oya hung around dangerous people or maybe got on the bad side of a killer?"

"I don't think that would be helpful."

This girl really needed to figure out sarcasm, because until she did, it was going to be hard to have a decent conversation with her.

We went back in the building to get to the front and from then on to the parking lot. The front of the building was decorated with some impressive bronze doors. Tourists were standing in front of them having their picture taken by a man with a badge on his vest reading VOLUNTEER.

It might be nice to volunteer at a place like this, if I could figure out how to do that, support me and Castro, and cope with all the new entanglements my life had suddenly presented me with. I'd never thought about doing volunteer work before, but suddenly it looked like a much nicer option than what I was afraid I was going to get.

We stepped outside and left the Visitor Center and its tourists and volunteers behind.

The sun beat down on us mercilessly, all the more so because it was now just after noon. I wondered how long the city was going to have to bake before we got any relief. I checked the weather app on my phone but it listed the weather for the next five days as being above ninety degrees. A heat warning announced in all caps that this was now officially the hottest September on record and it was only going to get worse.

And yet, I kept hearing the distant rolling of thunder. I glanced around but saw only one slight wisp of cloud to the south.

In other words, despite the rumblings in the sky, the city wasn't escaping this heat wave any time soon.

If the walk to the car was torturous, the air that rolled out of it as we opened the doors was worse. In a choice between standing in the oven and getting inside a hotter one, standing in the sun looked to be the better option.

But I wasn't going to be able to turn on the air conditioning from here. I got into the car, thankful once again I had cloth seats that would only heat up my ass and not give me second-degree burns. I flipped the a/c on and waited for Mia to settle into the car. We closed the doors and I put the car into gear.

"Belleville," I said, hoping to elicit more directions.

"Tark's Pizza. It's on the main street near where they have the art show every year."

"Never been there."

"You should go. The art is so unusual and interesting."

"Does Oya like that, too?"

"She goes, but only because I like it so much."

That made me like Oya a little better. I wasn't sure how I felt about immortals that took lovers for a few years and abandoned them, but at least Oya tried to take an interest in the things Mia wanted to do while she was with her.

"Head down I-255 to Highway 15 and go east."

I followed her directions and soon enough we were parked on the street near an unprepossessing brick building whose name was painted on the front in great swooping letters that seriously needed to be repainted.

Even this close to noon, the place sported empty tables and a television tuned to golf which even the employees weren't watching.

"Hi," said the cute teenaged girl at the host's stand. She wore a bright red shirt that said *Pizza is Life So Eat Tark's to Live.* That seemed a bit long for a slogan, but hey, it wasn't my business. "Two for lunch?"

Mia nodded. "Yes."

The girl showed us to a table by the window, where we could look out onto the street.

"Tina will be right with you," said the girl.

"Could we have Jordan?" asked Mia. "I'm sure Tina is lovely, but Jordan's...a friend of a friend."

The girl looked a little put out, but shrugged. "Sure. I'll let him know you're here."

I opened my menu, determined to stay out of whatever discussion Mia planned to have with Jordan.

A somewhat portly man emerged from the back a few moments later. He held his waiter's pad between his left arm and his chest. His arm ended just below the elbow. In his right hand, he carried a pen. He wasn't as midnight black as Oya, but his skin tone was dark enough that his bright blue eyes stood out. They were mesmerizing.

He did a noticeable double-take when he saw Mia, but he covered it quickly and made his face blank.

"Good afternoon, ladies," he said in a practiced monotone as he approached our table. "What can I get you to drink?"

"Just water for me," said Mia. She smiled at Jordan slightly, but he did not respond.

"Make that two."

Jordan nodded and walked away.

I wasn't even sure I knew Oya's type, but Jordan did not seem to be it. My face must have reflected my thoughts, because Mia said. "He's different now. Since being in the Army. Two tours in Afghanistan. That's where he lost his arm."

"That was after..." I couldn't say "Oya moved on to someone else" out loud, but Mia knew what I meant. If I were her, I would spend part of every hour of every day thinking about the coming inevitability.

I couldn't help myself. "So, how do you even know about him? You don't, I don't know, hang out, or something, right? That would be weird."

"I hardly think you're in a position to judge what's weird," she said. "No, we don't *hang out*. But I have...met him. Sort of."

What could I say to that? It made me appreciate Castro that much more. I didn't know if we'd be together for a lifetime, but at least our lives together weren't at the mercy of a self-imposed deadline.

It certainly made immortality, or at least being extremely long-lived, seem horrifically unappealing.

Jordan returned and deposited glasses of water in front of each of us.

"What would you like? Our special today is a large meat lover's pizza on a thick crust."

"That sounds good," I said. Mia only nodded.

"Fine."

"Jordan," said Mia hesitantly. "I need to speak with you for a few minutes before we leave. About...Babs." I wondered if she hesitated because she might have had no idea what Oya's name had been when she'd been with Jordan.

He retrieved the menus from us. "I've nothing to say to you."

"Wait," I said. "Why not?"

He leveled a gaze at me that would have withered most people, but, four nights ago, I'd faced down two immortal beings with only a mark on my palm as a weapon. Jordan was small potatoes next to that. Especially when wearing a ridiculous Tark's shirt.

He said, "When I got back home, I went by the house. I saw you there. I knew she'd move on, but I didn't think she'd rebound with a little white girl like you."

Mia looked shocked as Jordan walked away.

I couldn't help but think there was no way he wasn't spitting in our food. I moved my drink away, suddenly not thirsty any more.

"We could cancel our order and leave," I said.

"No, I don't want to do that."

Suddenly, a nasty thought crossed my mind. What would Mia be like once Oya left *her*? Bitter like Jordan? Or just sad, the way she was now? I could see it going either way.

Still, did that make Jordan a suspect in Oya's disappearance? I wondered who Ware would put on the list.

"Are there any Forlorn that Oya doesn't get along with? Anyone who'd want to cause her some inconvenience?"

She hesitated. "She despises Marveaux. There's another one, named something like Iya or Ishya, that she only mentioned once, but when she said his name, she spat it out and got this nasty look on her face. She hasn't mentioned others, but Ware might know."

"He seems to have checked the area for Marveaux," I said. "I've never heard of this other one. I'd certainly say Marveaux would be more than willing to kill, if what I saw the other day is any indication," I said with a shiver. I tried not to think about the demonic face and the brush of invisible feathers against my arm. I felt the feathers still, and unlike a feather pillow, the sensation had been anything but pleasant. Of course, that could have been because Marveaux had been trying to kill Castro at the time, and looked quite willing to include me as a bonus.

"I don't know him personally, thank God. When Babs came home to tell me she'd been with you that evening, and what you did, she seemed impressed by you, and disgusted by him. But she didn't say a lot. She usually doesn't. It's like she doesn't want me to be too afraid of them, like I'll leave her if I find out too much."

I could imagine. Actually, I couldn't imagine being immortal, but I thought I could imagine how unhappy that would make somebody after a while. Maybe unhappy enough to start trying to spread the malaise. And how better than to start murdering your target's ex-lovers? So could Marveaux be the one behind this?

Misery loves company, right?

9

In the end, we ate some pizza, put the rest in a box, and left. Right before we walked out, Mia said casually to Jordan, "Babs is missing. I don't know why. Keep your eyes open. Preston and Qiana are dead, but that might not be connected."

The way he looked at her, I knew he was thinking something along the lines of *I'm already dead.*

"So," I said when we got back to the car. I was planning to stop at the convenience store down the street to pick up a drink. Meat lover's pizza and nothing to drink was a bad combination. I'd only managed one piece of the pizza, too, though Mia had set to with a fierce hunger. She was so tiny, I assumed she didn't normally eat a lot. But who knew? Maybe she had a fantastic metabolism.

Or maybe she was stress eating.

"So, do I just take you back home now, or what?" As much as I was getting tired of Mia's melancholy, I wasn't looking forward to seeing Ware again with nothing to show for this little adventure except some incipient heatstroke.

"I..." She stopped. I looked up and my attention was riveted by the barrel of a gun pointing in the open door at Mia.

"I don't know what you thought you were accomplishing by coming here," said Jordan. "But you shouldn't have come."

"We're leaving," I said. "No one's bothering you again."

"Too late," he growled. "I don't know you—get lost. But *you*," he waved the gun in Mia's direction. "You get out of the car. You're coming with me."

"So you're the one?" she asked. "What did you do with her!"

Confusion gripped Jordan's face. "Do with her...Babs? I'd never hurt her. But if Preston and Qiana are also gone, then maybe *you're* the one who's doing it. After all, strange things happen around you."

"What strange things?" I asked. Was he right, or just paranoid from his wartime experiences? I was no expert on such things, but the gun pointing in the car was on the crazy side, as far as I was concerned.

I kept my eyes on the gun, but thought perhaps I should try to make a run for it. Maybe he'd be too focused on her to shoot at me, and besides, he'd just told me I could go, right? Maybe I'd make it to the restaurant and ask the other employees for help.

"Where are we going?" Mia asked.

"You're not going anywhere with him," I said as I put my hand on the handle of my car door. He had military training. How quickly could he change his target and get off a good shot? Probably quickly.

"It's okay," said Mia. She patted me on the leg. "I...I owe him. We both do." I assumed she meant she and Oya by "both," because I certainly didn't owe this gun-wielding psychopath a fucking thing.

"Stay here," I said. "Stay in the car. Do not go with the crazy guy with a gun!"

Both of them ignored me.

Jordan's shoulders drooped as Mia got out of the car and faced him calmly. He lowered the gun. A tear actually ran down his cheek.

"It's okay," she said.

The woman was certifiable. *She* was the one comforting *him* when he was the one threatening *her*? I didn't care he was crying—he was holding a gun and we were unarmed.

"Do not go anywhere with him," I yelled. I got out of the car but Jordan raised the gun again and I froze.

Mia stepped in between us. "Really, Teryl, it's all right. Jordan isn't going to hurt me. We're just going to talk."

Overhead, thunder rumbled even more strongly. Neither of the others appeared to notice.

"He could be a killer."

Mia shook her head. "I don't think so. Listen," she said condescendingly, "you're new to this. It was just last week you even learned that people like Babs and Ware exist. We've known about them far longer. And we love her. We've given her everything. We want to find her, don't we, Jordan?"

Jordan nodded, tears in his eyes. I forbore to say *Well, someone doesn't love her!* But I was sure Mia would ignore me.

"Come on, let Teryl go," wheedled Mia. "She doesn't really understand. I do. Besides, we should really talk. We owe you an apology, and more."

Jordan's tears kept coming. He nodded but was still hell-bent on his kidnapping scheme. "Leave your phone and come with me."

Mia reached into her pocket and tossed her phone onto the front seat of my car.

I watched helplessly as Mia followed Jordan to a run-down sedan that looked like it might originally have been silver. Now it was just dingy-looking and covered in dust and dried mud.

Mia got in the car without the slightest hesitation. I was disappointed; I'd thought perhaps she'd just been playing along, trying to protect me. Perhaps trying to wait until Jordan's attention was on opening the car doors and then she would run. But she sat primly in the passenger seat and never looked at me as Jordan drove away.

My phone rang. It was the bar's number.

I answered my phone. "Hello?"

"Any luck?" asked Ware.

"Not of the good kind."

"What does that mean?"

I took a deep breath. "Mia's gone."

"She's what?"

The phone gave an awkward series of raspy and crackling sounds and then Ware's voice took on an even deeper tone than usual. "Did I just hear you say *Mia's gone?* How could that happen?"

I quailed at the anger in his voice.

"I couldn't do anything about it," I jabbered, trying not to sound like an idiot. "We came to Tark's to talk to Jordan, but he refused to say anything until after we left. Then he threatened us with a gun. Mia said she'd go with him to explain everything. She said she owed him, that they both did. He cried. They left."

The line went silent. I waited while the a/c blasted me with cold air that, for the first time today, felt icy and unwelcome. My stomach turned in slow knots. I don't know what I could have done to protect Mia, but I should have done something. Ware had trusted me, and I had failed. I scanned the parking lot, as if that would do any good. A small wisp of smoke rose out of the area where Jordan's car had been. He must have tossed down a cigarette butt. Not only was he a kidnapper, but a litterbug.

"Just get back to the bar," Ware said at last, far too calmly. "We'll figure something out."

I said nothing.

"Teryl?"

I still remained silent. How could I go back to the bar where this immortal being waited for me. I didn't know if I could trust him, and I had no idea what was going on. I mean, *really* going on.

"Teryl? Just come to the bar. It's okay. We'll talk. We'll sort some stuff out, and we'll decide what to do."

The *we* was friendly and comforting. Not "I'll decide and tell you what to do."

"Okay," I said and hung up. I turned Nixie onto the street and headed back toward the highway.

Tens of thousands of starlings on the power wires watched me go. I felt like that was a bad omen, and I didn't even know why. It was like they were telling me to do something to save myself, and I didn't understand the message.

But how could I think of myself when Mia had just gone off with an armed crazy man? I wanted to pose that question to the damn birds. How could I live with myself when I was just driving away like nothing had happened?

I never had liked starlings, but now I really, really didn't like them.

The skyline of the city came into view and I left the farmlands and birds behind and crossed the PSB into Missouri. The sky continued to be cloudless but the roll of thunder only got louder.

8

I stared at the paint peeling on the black door of the bar. Ware had once suggested we find someone to redo it, but so far, the old stuff remained, flaking away in the sunlight, being rubbed away by drunk patrons at night who slid across it so they didn't fall face-down on the pavement.

I took a deep breath and opened the door. The familiar odors of alcohol, stale smoke, and old vinyl upholstery filled my nostrils. The smell of the Angels' Share. The smell every bartender at every such establishment knew intimately.

The tables and booths sported napkins neatly laid on the tables, but otherwise, they were empty. Of course, early afternoon was never a great time at the bar, but usually there was *someone* there.

Perhaps Ware had scared everyone off.

"Hey, Teryl," said Jeff, the afternoon bartender. He waved as I stepped into the bar. At least Jeff was an open, friendly face, and his smile made me smile. "Wasn't even sure you still worked here."

"Yeah, guess so."

"Then your shift isn't for half an hour," he said. "Except I think Boyle's coming in. Just need a place to hang out for a few minutes before work? Because there's a classier bar down the street."

I forced a laughed. No sense letting Jeff know anything was up. As far as I knew, he had no clue as to what Ware and Fish were, and wasn't the target of any crazies among the immortal crowd or those who wanted revenge on them. "No, Ware wanted to talk to me. It's not job-related, exactly. So he asked if I could come a little early."

That made Jeff's blond eyebrows go up. "Ware wants to talk you, but it's not about your job, exactly. Sounds mysterious."

I grimaced. "Yeah, probably not so mysterious when you get down to it, though."

"You'll have to let me know how it goes," he said. "I don't know anything about our boss. Think he's going to tell you his life story or something?"

"I hope not," I said. "I'm pretty sure I don't want to know."

Jeff's smile faded. He clearly didn't know how to take that comment. But what else could I say? I had no idea what Ware was likely to say, or even if it would be the truth. I guess I could trust he couldn't hurt me, because, you know, he didn't hurt people *without a reason*, and Mia had never heard of him harming someone he wanted to protect, and he wanted me to stick around, so I was probably safe. But that was as far as I could go. He could want me safe and still lie to me.

The door to Ware's office opened and there stood the man himself, looking much as he had this morning except that his expression was much more stormy. Physically, he was a solid presence, and strong as an ox; mentally, he was clearly in an unsettled mood. Alarmed, even.

Two hours ago he'd only seemed concerned. Either he knew more than he was telling, or he was more upset by Mia going off with Jordan than he really had a right to be. After all, he didn't know her that well.

Could she be someone he wanted to protect? I hadn't caught on to that this morning if it were true.

"Teryl will have more important things to do than gossip to you about this meeting, Mr. Olson."

Jeff, abashed, was suddenly occupied with wiping off the already-clean bartop. "Of course."

Ware stepped away from the door. I took a deep breath and stepped inside his office for the first time.

At first glance, there was no obvious reason for Ware to keep it off-limits to the staff, except out of a personal desire for privacy. But as I crossed the cluttered room, I realized my first glance had been wrong.

The haphazard pile of books on the desk looked like the old leather-bound tomes from movies, the sort that librarians or archaeologists were always checking for clues. What little gilded lettering was left on their spines was not in English, and what few words I could make out, though I couldn't understand them, did not look good: *maligno, monstrum, wyrm.*

A miniature human skeleton hung from a wire in the corner. I initially dismissed it as a Halloween decoration, but then I caught the glint of wires holding the joints together, and the yellowish color of the bones themselves. Small dark scraps of...something...hung off its ribs. The skeleton was also missing two teeth. How many Halloween decorations were so elaborate as to have individual teeth? But how many human skeletons were only a foot tall? And had skeletal wings attached to the back, as if Ware were displaying the remains of some tiny angel.

A small leather valise sat near the skeleton, open as if Ware was prepared to pack some things in it, but hadn't done it yet. I shuddered to remember the sack Oya had carried for Ware the other night, the one that had contained what I was sure had been a human soul.

A human soul that had been shredded. Destroyed. I forced that thought away.

The room was filled with the scent of mildewed ancient books and something dry and brittle, like old leaves in a basement stairwell. Instinctively, I knew I did not want to know what that smell belonged to. My skin crawled and I resisted the urge to start scratching at nothing.

Something moved in the corner but I'd seen enough. I sat down on the couch where Ware indicated, and did not look around. My boss settled himself on the couch next to me, just close enough to give the impression of an intimate conversation, but not close enough for us to touch. I was grateful for that. Ware had put his hand on my shoulder last week, and it had not been the comforting gesture I was sure it had been meant to be.

He took a deep breath, then another. I got the feeling he had no idea what to say, and for a moment, I found that more heartening than anything else. Whatever weirdness was going on, at least my boss was at a loss to explain it, or at least how to *begin* to explain it.

"Do you know what's going on? Did you hurt Oya? Preston? Qiana? Did you make Jordan do something with Mia?" Might as well ask straight-out, even if doing so made my voice shake and my knees quiver.

Ware's jaw dropped for a moment in a gesture that would have seemed comical coming from someone else. He cleared his throat and ran a hand through his white hair. "Fuck, Teryl, you'd really ask that?"

I clenched my hands into fists and hoped he didn't notice my bald, and more than likely stupid, attempt at being brave. "Why not? I think you know more about what happened with Oya than you've said. I think you haven't told Mia what you know. And I think you know something about what Mia thinks she owes Jordan, so much so that she'd get in a car with him and go somewhere, at gunpoint, and not even seem upset about it."

Ware looked stunned a moment longer, then collapsed into a pained laugh. "Oh, Teryl." He paused to catch his breath and leaned back against the arm of the couch, seemingly more relaxed than before.

I wasn't sure that was a good thing.

"Something has happened to Oya," he said. "But I'm afraid it may be partly my fault. Not Jordan's, not Marveaux's."

He fidgeted, fingers tapping relentlessly against his thighs.

I was reminded of how I met her the other night on Hall Street.

"She's doing something for you. A favor or an errand, whatever you want to call it."

He looked at me out from under his eyebrows. "Mia couldn't have told you that. She doesn't know."

"It just stands to reason," I said. "That's what she was doing the other night. But that errand didn't go the way it was supposed to. Now she's gone again, and you think it might be your fault."

"*Partly* my fault," he said. "The errand wasn't dangerous."

"But it may have exposed her to danger."

He shrugged.

"What was she doing?"

"You wouldn't understand."

"Try me."

He smiled, and it actually seemed genuine. It made him seem years younger. "Not today. My fear is that another one of us would have liked to send someone on the same errand, and decided that intercepting Oya was better than doing it themselves."

"So it *is* dangerous?"

He shrugged again. "More like not all of us have the same skills, as we talked about this morning. Oya is useful for more than directing lightning. Someone else may have decided they want what I want, and it wouldn't have been hard to figure out who I'd send out on the search."

"She's like a bloodhound for you."

He had the grace to look slightly embarrassed. "For lack of a better word, yes. She finds things for me."

"And the thing she was to find, that's what you don't want to tell me about."

"Basically."

"And now something's happened and you're happy to let Mia believe it might be a human who's after Oya?"

"Well," he said somewhat defensively, "it might be. Just like I might send *you* out on an errand, another Forlorn might send another human out. Just because Oya's missing doesn't tell us if who came for her was human or Forlorn."

I sighed. "So how many of you are there? And how many of them want what you want? How many of them might hold grudges against Oya?"

"Once we were legion," he said. "Now there are probably only a few dozen. I'm not even sure of the exact count."

"So you do you eventually die?" Looked like Pellagrio might have been lying to us. Not really surprising.

He looked uncomfortable again. "We retire, and that's all I'm saying about that right now. We should be looking for Mia."

"But not Oya?"

"If you know anything about us now, you should know we're immortal and damn near impervious to anything humans can dream up. Oya might be imprisoned somewhere, but she's not dead."

So maybe Pellagrio hadn't been lying. I wondered what Ware would make of Pellagrio's story.

"But you *can* die."

"Why would you say that?"

"Because I heard that today. I heard that one of you did die, and the consequences for the world were very bad."

He stared at me, but unlike Pellagrio, who made everything stand still, Ware's lips trembled and the thing in the corner hissed. I wanted to get out of here badly but instinct warned me to stay put. I did not want to anger whatever was in the corner.

Despite my fear, I felt reluctant to throw Pellagrio under the bus for giving me information Ware did not seem to want me to have. So I clamped my mouth shut and waited.

"Did you do the killing?" I asked.

"What? No! Did someone say that? Who was it!" Ware blanched and seemed genuinely upset. "No, of course not. She was..." He spread his hands in a gesture of surrender and helplessness. His expression fell and I couldn't help a sudden stab of pity. He hadn't killed this other fallen angel. His whole body seemed to grow smaller just thinking of her being dead.

"You loved her," I said quietly.

He was silent for several very long seconds and his gaze dropped to his lap, where his hands twitched as if he wanted to strangle someone but didn't know who to turn his anger on. Finally, he sighed.

"Several of us did. Her loss was...immeasurable. Still, she's not a discussion for today. Today we have to get Mia back."

"Why?"

He sat forward and I leaned back at the change in his body language. He had gone from mournful to aggressive in a moment. My heart pounded and my mouth was suddenly dry.

"Because Little Girl will be counting on it."

I felt like a two-year-old but I was tired of half-answers. "Why?"

A look of puzzlement crossed his face. "It's not enough that she's in danger?"

"I don't know that she's in danger," I said, though I was sure he was right. I just wanted him to come out and give a complete fucking answer for once. "And she told me herself that she knows Oya will move on to another lover someday. Maybe someday soon."

"Not too soon," said Ware. "She'll want to stay once the baby's born."

"Once the...what? Mia's pregnant? How can that happen?"

Shock caught me by surprise, but as I thought about it, I realized I should have known. The longing look at children, the appetite, the tiredness and inability to take the heat of the day. Hell, even Ware's solicitous helping her out of the booth earlier today should have been a clue.

"You have enough information. You should be able to put it together."

I exploded. "Who said I *wanted* to put it together? Why can't you just answer the damn question?"

"Because there's so much!" he shouted.

I winced and wondered if Jeff had heard that.

"*Because over and over again, the world changes,* and the people you care about die. There's no escape from it. Never. And no way to die. So we look for ways out. We're always looking for a way out."

The grief and longing in his voice froze my heart; it took several long moments for it to start beating again.

A vision came to mind of Marveaux in the crypt trying to create some kind of portal. "So that's what was going on with the crystal. With Marveaux and Garnett. They wanted out."

Ware nodded. "We all do. We've been here *so long*. And home is...is no longer where it was. We can never go home. We can only move on."

"And making portals is some kind of way to do that?"

"We call them sinkholes. I don't know if I can explain to you what they are right now, but I'm sure Little Girl isn't in one."

"And how is that?"

He refused to meet my eye.

"And how is that?" I repeated.

"Because there's only one in St. Louis, and it belongs to me."

Oh fuck. I didn't even know what that meant, exactly, but it couldn't be good, could it?

I decided to get the conversation back on track. Back to the matter at hand.

"Do you have some kind of plan? For finding Mia, I mean."

"I don't suppose Jordan announced where he planned to take her."

"No," I said, "though Mia seemed determine to make him aware that something had happened to Oya. If anything, I'd expect her to take him to Cahokia."

"Do you think he'd go?"

I thought of the sad look on his face when Mia had said they loved Oya. He had nodded. He loved her. He was jealous of Mia, but he still loved Oya. If she were missing, I bet he'd go to Cahokia to help find her.

My main concern was that he would hurt Mia first, and *then* go looking for Oya.

"I bet Jordan will be at Cahokia sometime today," I said. "But Mia? That I don't know. I can't even guess. Shouldn't we call the police?"

"What would you like to tell them?"

"That a guy with a gun got a woman into a car and drove off! That wouldn't even be revealing anything weird, and it's what happened."

"Could you explain to them why you left the scene to come here? Why you haven't called them already?"

I mulled that one over. "Maybe I was afraid?"

"After he left?"

My shoulders sagged. "I don't know what to do. I'm no good at lying and this is..." I spread my hands helplessly.

Ware put a hand on my knee briefly, then sat back. "You go back to Cahokia. You look for Mia, and if you find Oya, so much the better. You have a weapon in my mark: use it. It gives you the ability to injure us, though until you learn to focus its power, its ability to help you is limited."

"It hurt Marveaux."

"Yes, though that was a special circumstance, and you had help from the...scrap...Oya gave you."

"Scrap?"

All over again, something moved out of the corner of my eye and a dry scuttling sound came from behind me.

"Don't mind him," said Ware. "He's harmless as long as I'm here."

I shuddered. As much as I wanted to turn around to see what was making the noise, my gut was telling me to get out, to get away from it.

"One day you'll be able to control him, I have no doubt," said Ware, "but not today. Now, hold up your right hand."

I did so. Ware took a deep breath. "Okay, so think about hitting me. Think about focusing the strength of your arm and your shoulder into your palm."

That sounded ridiculous, but I got the idea I wasn't getting out of his office without doing what he said, and the sooner I was out of here, the better.

I thought about pulling my hand back and then swinging it forward, toward Ware's face. I didn't move my hand, but I thought very hard about what it would feel like for my palm to connect with his cheek. Just as it had felt earlier today with Pellagrio.

My palm started to itch and my fingers twitched involuntarily.

"Good," said Ware. "Like that. If you can focus that feeling when you want to, you should be able to stun any of us for a few seconds at least. That may not seem like much, but it's more than most people can do."

"Fine," I said, just wanting to get out of this office, out of the bar, and back our under the sunlight. "I can go to Cahokia, and I can hit one of you in the face, assuming I'm standing that close to one, and maybe stun them for a few seconds. So...any other advice before I go?"

"Don't go alone."

I laughed. "Who do I take, then? Fish? He got shot last time. You? How often do you even leave the bar? Lucy? She doesn't know me and doesn't seem too concerned, if this morning is any indication. *Jeff?* There's literally no one for me to go with who would have a reason to go, who knows what's going on, and who would care about me or Mia."

Ware seemed at a loss for words. As annoying as that was in this situation, it was also a bit gratifying. He wasn't all-seeing or all-knowing. He could just pull off the appearance of being so, at least most of the time.

"Take Yama," he said at last.

I shook my head. "I've never even spoken to him. Does he know Mia? Does he had a reason to come along?"

"Yes," said Ware simply. "He's off somewhere this afternoon, but he'll be reachable. I'm going to ask him."

Ware pulled out his cell phone and made a call. I waited, still itching to get out of this office.

I'd never seen Yama any closer than across the bar. He'd come in before closing sometimes to drink with Oya, Lucy, Ware, and Truck. As far as I could tell, the members of this little drinking club were Ware's closest companions. Or friends, if these creatures had things like that. If Ware were right and there were only a few dozen of them in the world today, you'd think they'd have reasons to be tight.

But, then, with some of them being homicidal maniacs like Marveaux, perhaps not.

Yama was not much taller than me, and plump, but light on his feet. I had assumed he was Asian, but since I now knew he was an immortal creature from another dimension, something that had once had wings and might best be described in common parlance as a fallen angel, I knew he wasn't. He wasn't human, or even from this planet.

How these people decided what they would look like was beyond me. Perhaps along with changing their names every few years, they changed appearance, too.

Maybe he'd looked like a small red-headed Irish woman a few centuries ago. How would I ever know? Why would I even care? For now, he affected the appearance of a somewhat overweight Asian man in a mustard jacket. That was the Yama I would have to deal with today.

Ware spoke to him on the phone in a language I did not recognize, which wasn't that hard to do. My exposure to foreign languages was limited. On the streets of St. Louis, I'd heard a bit of Spanish, and some Bosnian, but not much else. I didn't have friends from other countries. I didn't watch movies with subtitles. I led a fairly sheltered, insular life.

Which had suited me just fine.

Ware put the phone down. "He's already in Illinois, at some kind of flea market or something. The man can't stop shopping for knick-knacks. Anyway, he'll meet you there."

"Okay. Anything I should know about him? Fish is good at mind-reading, and you can make marks on people's hands. What can Yama do?"

"He's often good at sensing where others of our own kind are," said Ware, which made me wonder why Yama hadn't gone looking for his drinking pal Oya the moment he heard she had gone missing.

Ware's expression made me stop. He was debating telling me something else, something I probably needed to know.

"And...?" I prompted.

"And he's very good with poison."

I almost laughed. If a situation developed at Cahokia between me and Jordan, or me and another one of Oya's exes, I doubt poisoning them would help. I'd need someone with fighting skills, or serious powers of persuasion. Poison was a stealth weapon.

People joke about taking a knife to a gunfight, but taking poison to any kind of fight sounded just as ridiculous.

But Ware's face was far too serious to allow laughter. He thought Yama would be useful. He should know. After all, they'd been acquaintances for thousands of years, right?

"I'll...I'll see you later," I said. The rustling sound behind me got louder. I stood and headed for the door. Whatever it was on the floor ran by me; it brushed against my ankle. Where it touched me, my skin reacted as if to an electric shock. I yelped and couldn't get out of the office fast enough.

9)

Jeff was pouring a drink for Fish, who sat at the bar now, but I didn't pause to wave to either of them. I needed to get outside. Now.

Once I got to my car, I got in, started the a/c, and did my best to calm down and take stock of the situation. When I'd gotten up this morning, I had looked forward to a slow day of sitting around the apartment *not* going to work, and spending an evening with Castro curled up on the couch watching a movie. Something funny.

Now...I was neck-deep in missing people and fallen angels and crazy shit that clearly wasn't going to give me some decent introspection time. In fact, from now on, when a character on TV or in a movie told another they needed time to "process" something, I was going to yell at them and throw something.

"Process" crap, my ass. What really happened was that stuff threw itself at you so quickly, you only had time to try to keep afloat long enough for someone to throw you a rope.

Or just drown. Which is what I felt I was going to do if I went to Cahokia. Honestly, the temptation to go home, crawl under the covers, and wait for Castro to come home to tell me everything would be all right, was there, but I knew it was just a pipe dream.

My old life could never be reclaimed. These people and their circle of human acquaintances were part of my life now. I was going to have to find a way to cope with that, and do it well enough to survive.

I thought about Mia and her blond curls and melancholy. I thought about Jordan and his shock at finding himself replaced in Oya's affections by Mia. They had to find ways to cope, too. But I knew in my heart it was going to be a rougher road for me.

Damn it all.

Besides, could I look at myself in the mirror tomorrow if I fled now? If I went home and left Oya lost, Mia crying and kidnapped, and Jordan, used and discarded, now a kidnaper and maybe worse?

I wanted to say *yes*. Yes, I could live with anything if I could just retreat and keep myself and Castro safe. We'd have each other, and all the fallen angels in the world could just go fuck themselves.

It was tempting, but it was fantasy. Someone like Marveaux would pull me in again, or hound me, or kill me. Castro would still be in danger.

On the other hand, the weird hallucination at Cahokia had been something I didn't care to repeat. What if that happened again? What if happened a lot now that my life was touched by the supernatural?

But even if I left, would it stop? I'd been touched now. No going back, not from the moment I took this job months ago. If I were being honest, I had to realize there'd never really been a choice. If Ware sought out the Lost like me, he would have crossed my path eventually.

I'd been born to this, whether I liked it or not.

I couldn't go home.

I put Nixie in gear and headed back across the river. On the way, I wondered what Yama would consider "meeting me there." The parking lot? The Visitor's Center? One of the mounds?

At least he'd be fairly easy to spot from a distance. No one else was likely to be wearing his favorite color.

The parking lot was nearly empty so I was able to find a spot which offered at least a modicum of shade and hiked to the Visitor's Center. If anything, the day had heated up more than ever. I would not be surprised to find out we'd surpassed the record temperature for this date.

Around me, the day was still and very quiet. I guessed it was too hot for the birds, and even the insects. The air shimmered above the parking lot and sidewalks without even the slightest breeze to displace it. I was soaked with sweat before I got halfway to the Visitor's Center.

A smiling white-haired volunteer greeted me on entering. "Welcome to Cahokia!" He held out a brochure.

"Thanks," I said. I held up a hand to forestall him, since he seemed about to launch into some kind of welcome speech. "I'm actually here to meet someone. Have you seen an Asian gentleman in a yellow coat?"

The man thought about it a moment, then shook his head. "All kinds of people in today, but I don't recall anyone by that description. Perhaps he hasn't arrived yet."

"Perhaps not. When do you close?"

"Five o'clock."

I glanced at my phone. It was almost three thirty. "I guess I'll wait for him in here," I said.

"We have an orientation movie that's about fifteen minutes long," said the volunteer. "We'll be starting one up shortly."

"No thanks," I said. "I just need to wait for someone." I spotted a bench near the diorama I'd noticed earlier. "I'll just sit there."

"Sure. If you need anything, let us know."

"Thanks." I walked toward the bench and sat facing the bronze doors. Now that I had a good look at them, I realized they depicted the natives of Cahokia in their city with their mounds and the wildlife that surrounded them. They looked suspiciously like the people in the hallucination I'd had. I didn't care for that at all.

After a while, staring at the doors grew dull. I contemplated going in the gift shop, or checking out the displays in the museum, but either of those options would take me out of sight of the front doors. Perhaps it would be best to go outside.

Or I could call Ware, and he could call Yama. Too bad Ware hadn't given me Yama's contact information, or I could text him myself. Of course, that presumed I wanted to know how get in touch with more of these creatures.

Having a bunch of fallen angels in my contact list was not high on my list of priorities.

The door opened. Maybe Yama had finally arrived. But no. It was someone else entirely.

My mouth dropped open as Castro walked into the Visitor's Center. He was approached by the same volunteer who had approached me, but Castro waved him off with a quiet "thanks" and came over to me. He seemed a bit puzzled but strangely excited.

"Hey," he said as he sat down beside me and gave me a kiss on the cheek. "I didn't know you liked to hang out here."

"I...what? I don't hang out here. I've never been here before today. What are *you* doing here?"

He looked confused. "You texted me and said to come meet you here. Said you needed help finding someone? That sounded interesting and mysterious. Is this an escape room adventure? You round up a few friends and work through a puzzle of some kind?"

"I did not text you and this isn't a game." I showed him my phone, which did not, of course, show any outgoing texts from me to him.

"Huh," he said. "Well, then what are you doing here, and who wants me to show up if not you?"

"I don't know." But I had my suspicions. Who could it be but Ware? He hadn't wanted me to be here alone, and perhaps he knew that Yama would not rush to join me, or skip out entirely. He wouldn't have any qualms about putting Castro in harm's way. The mark on my palm was something he'd done to protect *me*, but that didn't mean his favor extended to anyone else.

"And why are you here then? Does this have something to do with the other night, the one I can't remember?"

I opened my mouth to say "no" but I couldn't do it. I couldn't lie to him.

"So it does," he said. "I keep having weird dreams, and you've been staying home and acting like something drastic happened. I've been letting this go on without commenting as much as possible, because I thought you needed some time. But now someone's texting me as you? You're sitting someplace you've never been before to do something you weren't going to tell me about. So, what gives?"

I dropped my gaze to my lap and noticed I had my hands clenched together, knuckles white, skin especially pale.

"It's hard to say," I said at last. "I don't really understand it myself. What do you remember? What do you dream?"

"Mostly something about being trapped somewhere. And maybe...something happening underground? I know Fish and I went somewhere, but it gets fuzzy after that. I feel like I should be able to remember more, but it's like there's something in my head preventing it. Every time I try to remember, my thoughts slide somewhere else."

I reached for his hand and held it tightly. How could I explain something I didn't understand myself? "Fair warning, it's really crazy shit. But, as far as I can tell, real shit."

That got his attention. Castro had always liked tales of the unexplained and couldn't get enough stories about ghosts, aliens, lake monsters, and anything else that seemed spooky and mysterious.

"Okay," he said. "Lay it on me."

I took a deep breath. "The bottom line is, there are these beings, like interdimensional creatures or, since they apparently once had wings, angels. My boss is one of them. Fish is one, too. Another one kidnapped you and Fish and tried to sacrifice you to open some kind of doorway to another dimension."

He didn't even take a moment to think about that. Maybe years of watching shows on UFOs and ghosts and Bigfoot had prepared him for something like this. Or maybe he remembered more than he thought, and had more or less figured it out already. "But you stopped him or her. Or them. Obviously, or I wouldn't be here."

I nodded. I turned over my hand. "This is one of the ways Ware helped me: he wrote his name, his original name, on my hand in marker, but I bled on it and then hit the guy trying to kill you. That apparently fused the mark with my body, so now it's part of me."

"Cool."

I was miffed he didn't seem to be taking this seriously. I'd just told him a powerful interdimensional creature had tried to kill him, and his response was *cool*.

"Not really," I said. "It was fucking scary and we almost didn't get out of there with our lives. Today, I'm looking for a girl named Mia, who is pregnant and missing. Her lover is another one of these beings, and she's missing, too."

Castro digested that for a few seconds. "If her lover's female, how does the pregnancy come about? Are these angel-things even able to breed with humans if they come from another reality?"

"I don't know, and I don't know. All I do know is I'm waiting for another one of them to show up to help out. I've never spoken to him before, though I've seen him at the bar sometimes. He calls himself Yama. Ware thinks he can help find Oya and Mia."

The doors opened again and Yama came through. He walked right by the brochure-laden volunteer and he strode over toward us, calm and completely unhurried. His short hair was neatly combed and he appeared unfazed by the heat. Under his standard yellow jacket he wore a brown polo shirt and khakis. This guy liked the warm colors, I guess.

"Hello," he said in a deep resonant voice as he got closer. "Teryl," he held out his hand and I shook it. His handshake was firm and his skin slightly cool. Perhaps heat didn't affect him the way it did humans. "I don't know this young man."

"I'm Castro." He stood and shook Yama's hand.

I stood as well. This close, I realized we were equal in height, which made Castro the tallest by several inches. "Ware told you about what's going on?"

He nodded. "Insofar as anyone knows what's going on, yes, I suppose he did. So shall we get started?"

"Okay." We walked out the back doors of the building. "Ware said you can find things."

Yama nodded. "Not the Lost, like you. That is Ware's power," he said with a smile. "But I can find members of my own kind. Usually. Some of them are good at hiding, even from me."

"What do we need to do to help?" asked Castro.

"Merely let me concentrate as we walk." I took that to mean we should shut up. I slowed down and let Yama get ahead of us. Castro slowed down, too.

"He's one of these angels?" he asked in a low voice.

"Yep."

"He knows you?"

"I told you, I've never spoken with him. He comes to the bar to drink with Ware and some others."

"I gotta start coming to this bar."

Yama's stride got longer.

"Maybe he's picked up the scent," said Castro.

"Maybe. And you shouldn't come to the bar. You aren't even supposed to be *here*."

He looked hurt, and I recalled Mia saying how I would need to tell him what was going on for his own protection.

"But you were going to fill me in eventually," he said, as if he could read my thoughts. "I nearly got killed the other night and you weren't going to leave it like that forever, right?"

I took a deep breath. "I don't know. It's not like I've got a manual. There's no *The Ten Best Things To Do When the Supernatural Enters Your Life* book. I wouldn't even go into work to talk to Ware about it. You yourself just said you were giving me time to work through some stuff, and I guess Ware has, too, since he didn't call me to see why I wasn't at work. But that doesn't mean I've magically figured it all out."

Yama held up a hand. By now, we had reached the two large mounds behind the Visitor's Center. To the left was the path that Mia and I had taken to the smaller mound where we had met Pellagrio.

My head felt fuzzy. I turned to the left. Ahead of me were hundreds of people with torches. The trees faded away until only their shadows were left; instead, I stood in the middle of a dusty, hard-packed surface where a crowd milled around in excitement and fascination. Beyond the people with torches...

"Teryl?"

I blinked. The scene in front of me wavered but now I saw Yama in his mustard jacket. He was faint, like an afterimage, but he was there. He stared at me intensely.

Another voice. "What's going on?" Castro. I held out my hand and someone grabbed it. My heart beat with fear but at least I wasn't alone.

"Teryl," said Yama slowly. "Don't fight it. Use it. Let her draw you to herself."

That didn't make any sense. I didn't feel drawn. I just felt confused. Where was I?

"Castro?" I said in a panic. "Castro, help me!"

He squeezed my hand.

"Keep hold of her," said Yama. His voice was faint, as if I were hearing it from far away, and yet his hazy image stood only a few feet from me. "We need to know what she's seeing."

"Talk to me, sweetie," said Castro.

He knew how much I hated that pet name. "Shut up," I said.

"Yep, got her," said Castro's voice with some satisfaction, though it was getting more hollow. Instead, from ahead of me, I heard singing. It grew louder.

"So what do you see?" asked Yama.

"I'm not sure. Lots of people are gathering. They're focused on the area ahead of us. There's singing and I think a few people are dancing, and maybe...chanting? I don't know; it's all confused."

"See what they're interested in."

I didn't want to. I really didn't want to. These people weren't mine. I didn't know their language. I didn't know why we were all gathered here and focused on the area ahead of us.

I wanted to leave.

Someone squeezed my left hand. "Come on, Teryl, I'll go with you," said Castro. He gave a gentle tug.

But I couldn't go. Something had arrived, or woken, or had suddenly noticed me. I didn't know which. But I was in its sights now. I felt it looming over me and around me.

You came, said a voice from behind me. Oya. Her voice was full of longing. *You came.*

I spun around but I didn't see her. In front of me were more dark people in skins and feathers and body paint, some laughing, some singing, some looking stressed or unhappy. But all focused on the area where the dancing and chanting was coming from.

"Teryl, what the hell?" asked Castro.

Arms wrapped around me. Cold wet arms that squeezed and moved over my body. I tried to pull away but I couldn't.

Fingers explored every inch of my torso but I could not evade them. My soul shuddered. This was a thousand times worse than any groping in a bar. Here, I could not fight back.

The hands kept caressing me but now I realized they had ceased to be *outside* my body. I felt no pain, but the sensation of fingers fondling my organs made me twitch and scream.

"Stop, just stop," I said. I begged. But the hands continued to be inside me and then pulled on me. The body behind me began sliding into me, as if I were an old shirt and something wanted to wear me.

"No, no, no," I whispered, but even that was taken from me as the being slid into my head and mind. All of a sudden, the phrase *riding horses* made more sense to me. I was being ridden, used like a puppet.

Used.

I tried to scream, but had no control over anything. I could only exist, and wait, while an alien clutched me, body and soul.

We have to save the thunder, said Oya's voice in my head. Or my voice. I couldn't tell.

"Who said that?" asked Castro. He sounded alarmed. Good for him; that made two of us. "That didn't sound like Teryl, but it came from her."

"Teryl, you have to maintain some control," said a voice deeper than Castro's. Who was that? Didn't I know that voice?

I looked around and saw him. *Floating Embers of the Transcendent Desert.*

"Sapphire at the Eye of the Storm," he said in response to that thought, responding in a language so ancient no human had ever known it. "So, we're using our old names now?"

I saw in him a strange double vision. In one version, he was shorter and rounder with black hair, deepest brown eyes and a smooth beardless face. In another, he was far taller, with flowing coppery tresses and skin of darkest bronze.

His face was longer than a human's, and fanged. His cheekbones jutted out and his eyes were larger than they should have been. He was vaguely humanoid, but clearly not human. The angles and planes of his face were no longer rounded, but severe and sharp.

But most importantly, behind him, he held his glowing golden wings high over his head. They were as magnificent as I remembered them.

My own shoulders were heavy with a weight I missed so much it hurt to even think of it. But here, in memory, I could see them just as they had been. I angled my wings around my shoulders; beautiful wings with dark blue feathers, the deepest, most beautiful midnight blue, each tipped in black. Greedily, I stared at them, drinking in the sight. It had been too long. Far too long.

For some griefs, time was not enough to assuage the pain. The loss of these wings haunted me every moment of my existence for a thousand centuries. But here, in the mists of memory, I could see them again. Feel the muscles that supported them rippling down my back.

Mine.

"Teryl, you have to come back, at least part of the way," said the gold-and-bronze figure in front of me.

"What's happening to her?"

"The Sapphire is riding her. That's not Teryl at the moment."

A pause, then "It's one of *you?*"

"Yes."

"She's possessed."

"For lack of a better word, yes."

I flapped my wings idly, wondering if I could fly in my memories. Around me, the shades of the people I'd occasionally visited, and accepted worship from, continued to move toward the mound ahead.

There had been a time when these people had done my bidding, and I had blessed them with my lightning. Lightning to start the sacred fires. Lightning to strike fear into the hearts of their enemies. My lightning.

Except that wasn't why I was here. The thunder was coming. I had to do something about the thunder.

My heart twisted in grief. I'd thought, if I couldn't have what I wanted so badly, maybe *she* could have what *she* wanted. I knew it was a bad idea, but it couldn't really be that dangerous, could it? *He* would never have to know I'd done it.

"Where is she?" I asked. We asked?

"Who?"

"Mia." I said the name softly, recalling her delicate face, her golden curls, the way she nestled against me in bed, the way her gentle teasing fueled my desire for her. She seemed so willowy and passive, but that wasn't her true nature. That was just the outer trappings. Inside, she had a core of iron, a strength that had attracted me to her. What she wanted, she got. And what she wanted was...

"Oya!" The voice was commanding. My attention snapped back to my winged companion. Anger had settled on his face, was evident in the way he canted his wings. He was furious. "This is enough. Tell us where you are and let her go."

Tell him where I was? Wait, where was I? Around me, the shadows of people who had been began screaming and running as fire raced through the crowd. Fire from lightning. My lightning.

Around me, everything burned.

Burning. Burning. Everything burns.

"She says things are burning, or something's burning. I don't understand it," said my companion to the other one, the one who held my left hand.

"It's awfully hot today."

"I do not think that is what she means. But I may be able to do something about this."

Before I could react, the winged creature in front of me reached out and grabbed my right hand. Pain shot up from my palm through my shoulder, up my spine, through every pore in my wings. It wrapped around my brain and seared its way through my eyes and mouth.

I tried to scream, but the pain had taken my breath. I lurched back, reclaiming both my hands. My wings, my beautiful wings! They faded into memory and the weight of them fell off my shoulders like an old coat sliding to the floor.

The loss of them, even the memory of them riding my shoulders, was so very painful. "You dare!" I screamed.

I wanted to curse him. But more words would not come.

I...wait, who was I? Teryl Gray. I was Teryl, a bartender, and an unwilling participant to whatever invasion this was.

"Get out of my head," I growled.

Not until I have what I want.

I held up my hands in front of my face. For a moment, they were dark like ebony and covered in bracelets, but that faded. They were much paler, and without any adornments, though the skin was sporting some redness after boiling under this hot sun today.

"Teryl? How are you doing?"

I glanced over at Yama. He looked normal once more, no bronze hair, no dark gold skin, no pure golden wings. Just a somewhat portly Asian guy whose round features were at odds with the angled creature he had just been in my memories.

But my will was still not entirely my own. I could not speak. Oya held my lips shut, clamped down on my vocal cords. This was not over between us.

Yama put his hands on each side of my face and stared into my eyes. "There's only so much I can do, and I can't take it back. And you still have to find out where Mia and Oya are."

You do it, I wanted to say. Hadn't Ware said Yama was good at finding others of their own kind?

"Normally, I could. But Oya's done something that's blocking me. And no, I'm not reading your mind. Your face tells me what you're thinking."

Great.

Find me. Find her.

Get out of my head first, bitch.

I got no response to that, but the steel trap on my mind wavered. Not due to me, but due to the pain in my brain and every joint. I felt it. But she felt it, too, and it hurt her more than it hurt me.

For once in my life, I didn't mind pain so much, so long as my attacker suffered more than I did. Let Oya stew. I was here to help, and she was holding on to my voice and my mind. Violating my soul. For that, she could suffer untold agonies as far as I was concerned.

As will you if you do not save the thunder.

What does that even mean?

He is coming. He will kill her if we do not do something, and we must save him.

I had no idea what that meant, but my attention was snared again by the mound in the distance. The shadowy figures of Cahokia's past had almost entirely faded away so that most of what I saw was yellowed grass, a small rise in the level of the ground, and trees drooping from the heat.

And a thin line of black smoke, rising up from behind the mound.

Save them.

I ran forward, toward the smoke.

11

"Where are you going?" shouted someone from behind me.

"There's a fire," said someone else.

I paid those voices no heed. The wisp of smoke was joined by a second, and then by a third. Someone was setting fire to the woods on the other side of the mound.

My heart pounded. With everything so dry, this entire area would go up in minutes. But I knew I had to get to the fire. That was where I would find my love, though why she would be here, I did not know.

So the unwelcome tenant in my head had violated my mind, but wasn't reading my memories. That was something, I guess.

Or she was just momentarily distracted, because I could sense my thoughts were more my own than they had been since I had first seen the shadows of Cahokia some minutes ago. Oya's thoughts were only on those she loved.

The baby! We must get to Mia and the baby! Oya's thoughts slithered around in my mind and thrashed about in a helpless rage and panic.

"Stop that!" I screamed at her. Having her in my head made me feel, not just violated and sick, but off-balance. I ran carefully, because I felt at any moment, I would simply tumble over from being top-heavy. Two people in one head was a problem.

Not for me.

"Shut up."

I had arrived at the mound. More smoke rose from the woods just beyond. Its acrid smell was beginning to infiltrate the area. Several deer and one surprised-looking turkey fled the woods and ran across the trail, completely oblivious to the people approaching them.

Fire frightened everyone and everything.

Keep going keep going keep going!

"I said shut up. How do you even know Mia's here?"

She's here she's here.

The mantra continued. I slowed and stepped carefully into the woods. The ground was spongy, even after this heat wave. It must be terribly wet at most times if now, after a summer of no rain, it still felt like walking on a foam mattress.

Hurry!

"You want me to fall and hurt myself, and I'll be no good to you. So do us both a favor and shut up and let me do this."

That worked. Hallelujah. No voice responded in my head, no more orders speared my conscious mind.

The woods were close and beginning to fill with smoke. I'd be crawling soon to stay under it. For a moment, I thought about turning around, but if I did that, I was sure Oya would regain control. Anything to keep me moving forward, toward the fire. Why she thought that would get me closer to Mia was still a mystery.

The smoke grew thicker. I put my hands over my mouth and hoped that would help a little.

I passed a small tree whose twigs were on fire. Every instinct in my body warned me to run away, but I kept on. One step. Two steps. Anything to keep my mind my own for as long as possible. If walking into a fire achieved that, then that's what I would do.

There. Just ahead. Did I spot a small foot? I had to push aside a tangle of brittle vines. They snapped in my hands and cut my arms, but I ignored that. I had to get to Mia.

She lay on her side on the soft ground, small cuts marking her bare arms and face. She had scrabbled through the vines, too. Her hair was full of brambles and her lips were pale.

Had Jordan shot her? Strangled her? She was so still. I rushed forward and put a hand lightly against her throat. She was warm and her heart beat strongly. Besides the few small abrasions and cuts, I saw no obvious injuries. Her breaths were shallow, but she seemed all right, at least as far as a cursory inspection went.

"Here!" I shouted. "I found her!"

"Oya?" said Yama.

"No, Mia."

Castro came and knelt by me. "Is she okay?"

"I think so. We have to get her out of here."

A bush nearby suddenly crackled into flame. I hadn't seen the fire get so close.

"Shit," said Castro. "That just burst into flames on its own."

I wasn't sure if that were comforting or not. So I hadn't missed the fire coming closer, but bushes that spontaneously burst into flames were nothing I wanted to mess with.

"Okay, we got to her, let's go." Castro reached for Mia, but the moment his hand touched Mia, he was flung backward. Thunder boomed overhead so loudly my ears rang.

"What was that?" asked Yama.

I turned around to see if Castro was okay, but an iron will in my head pulled me back to Mia. *Save her.*

"We're trying to." I couldn't move my head, so I shouted, "Is Castro okay?"

"Yes," said Yama. "What happened?"

"I got fucking shoved back by a...a shockwave...of some kind," said Castro in a dazed and frightened voice. "What the hell is going on here?"

"She keeps telling me we have to save the thunder. Does that mean anything to you?" I asked.

Yama came up to kneel beside me. "Perhaps. I would not think of Oya as being that stupid, but clearly, if she has done what I think she has, this is going to be a difficult pregnancy and a very special child."

"The woods are on fire, people," yelled Castro. "Do you really have time to debate this now?"

"Only the Lost can touch her in this condition," said Yama. "You'll have to pull her out."

"I'll do it," said another voice. I looked up into the face of Jordan. I jumped backward.

"You won't touch her!"

Yama got in between us. "Who is this?"

Beside me, another tree burst into flames.

"We really don't have time to argue," I said. "But he's the one who kidnaped her at gunpoint a couple of hours ago."

"It wasn't loaded," said Jordan. "I just wanted to talk to her. I wanted to find out what they did to me. She insisted we had to come here so we could talk. Then she fell asleep. The closer we got, the more I realized I had to carry her to where she wanted to go. We're not quite there yet. It's just ahead."

Jordan's face was dazed, his eyes slightly unfocused.

"Don't touch her!" I said in another's voice. Oya slammed her will down on mine again. "You will not harm her or the child."

"Child?" asked Jordan. "What child?"

My heart froze. How had Jordan carried Mia here if only the Lost could touch her right now? He had to be Lost. So what he had wanted to talk to Oya and Mia about was...

You raped him. I thought as hard as I could to my unwelcome tenant. *He's the father of this baby and you possessed him. You can only possess the Lost. And now he can touch her when only the Lost can. You're a monster.*

I couldn't remember the last time I'd been so angry. Frightened, sure. Confused, certainly. But not consumed with soul-burning, gut-wrenching *fury*. That she and Mia would dare collude to invade someone's consciousness. That they would take him, and use him, and then toss him aside.

He agreed.

That had to be a bald-faced lie. Like you could explain to someone ahead of time what they were in for. How did you ask, "Hey, do you wanna fuck my girlfriend, the one I replaced you with, and I'll be shacking up in your head when you do it? Then is it okay if I toss you back on the street after?"

Like hell he did. Then why did he forget? Why did he have to ask Mia what happened? Why was the father of your baby working at a pizza joint while the two of you played house and prepared a nursery?

Her thoughts slithered around mine again, but now she was angry with me. *You dare question me!*

You bet I do. And judge you, too.

You have no right.

I felt her coiling in my mind to strike at Jordan. Exactly what she had the power to do through me, I didn't know and didn't want to find out. This had to stop right now.

"Jordan, get her out of here," I said before Oya could do something to him. "Yama, get Castro out, too. Oya and I have to have a chat."

No! screamed Oya in my mind as Jordan reached down, and with his good arm, scooped Mia off the ground. Damn, he had to be strong to do that. *He kidnapped her! He should never touch her. I'll kill him.*

You have to deal with me first, bitch.

I took a deep breath, held up my right hand, and slapped myself on the face.

I screamed as red howling pain flattened me against a tree and then slammed me to the ground.

"What the hell are you doing?" shouted Yama. "I didn't give you power to use it on yourself!"

"Get out of here," I growled. "If I can't find her body and slap her senseless, then this is the next best thing."

"Oya," he said as he turned. "I hope she makes you rue the day you ever tried to sire the Thunderer."

The sound of his footsteps faded. Thunder rolled all around us, and the tree I had just been flung into lit up with orange flame.

I must go to her. I must protect her.

"Fine job you've been doing, getting yourself lost, or kidnapped, or whatever," I said through gritted teeth. I coughed on the smoke. It burned my lungs and my eyes, but I wasn't moving from this spot. "And then turning Jordan into a victim—a guy you used to love, supposedly—so that now he's guilty of assault and kidnaping. I won't even pretend to know what Yama meant by what he said. All in all, it sounds like you've been a very bad girl, and if I have to hold you here to burn you out of my head, then fine. You can stay lost, or dead, or whatever, forever. Let Ware find another pet errand-runner."

Another tree, and then another, were consumed with flames. The heat seared my skin and my heart beat with terror. Being burned alive was about the worst thing I could think of.

Except having my mind taken over and being an observer in my own head. I was me. I was Teryl Gray, and I would be in control of my own mind, or I would die here.

I only hoped I had the strength to back up that threat.

My cheek still stung. More than stung, actually. My fear of the fire had pushed that pain to the edge of my consciousness for a few moments, but my face *hurt*. Like I'd scraped off all my skin.

I had no clear idea of what Ware had done to my hand, but if this is the way it had made Marveaux or Pellagrio feel, I almost pitied them. My face throbbed and every tooth on that side of my skull throbbed with it.

Oya had had enough. I felt her clamping down on my mind again, but this time, I had more space than before. The pain from the slap was still strong enough to help me hold her back. I stepped closer to a burning tree, imagining myself throwing my arms around it, pressing my face into the fire, and letting it spread to my clothes and skin.

My knees were weak with terror. Could I really do that?

Thick black smoke billowed out of the woods to my left and rolled past me. I choked, unable to breathe the acrid air, and dropped to the ground.

I wouldn't have to walk into the fire if I died of smoke inhalation first. Of the two ways to go, I think I preferred the smoke. I took a deep breath and coughed violently.

No, said Oya. *Wait. Don't die. You have to get me out of here. You have to get me back to Mia.*

I couldn't speak through the coughing and gasping for air. I thought *I don't have to do squat for you.*

You don't want to die, she wheedled.

Damn straight I didn't want to die. But I wasn't going to be her pet bitch, either. My heart seized with the thought of never seeing Castro again. Of never going home again. Of never seeing our prickly little Petunia again.

My eyes teared up with more than smoke. Oya was right. I didn't want to die. But that thought wouldn't make me move from where I was.

Oya clearly read my continued intent to stay right where I was.

Go back toward the mound, she said at last in a defeated voice. *I swear on my own feathers, I will do as you bid if you find me and bring me back to my lover.*

Lovers, I thought as sharply as I could. She had professed to care for Jordan at one time. Now she said she loved Mia. Who knew what she really felt?

I crawled across the spongy forest floor, but wasn't sure I had the right direction. The skin on my palms blistered. The smoke surrounded me and cut me off from any visible landmarks.

This is the way. You can sense it if you try.

And I could. I knew to go just a little to the right. Once around a smoldering tree, I knew to adjust my course slightly to the left. I did not question how I knew these things. I only knew I was closer to Oya with every foot I went, and even deeper into the fire.

12

At last, I got to a spot where the prompts stopped. I had gone to the place Oya wanted me to be. I had no idea where that was, no way to escape once I'd done whatever Oya wanted me to do, but it was the right spot.

Climb.

Climb? In a fire? Through the smoke?

Climb.

I looked at the tree next to me. A few curlicues of flame had started at its base. If I climbed it, I would be trapped at the top of a burning tree.

Assuming I could even climb it with all this smoke. I'd more likely die of smoke inhalation and just drop to the ground. The only good side to that I could see was it was likely to be a more merciful death than burning in the fire itself.

Unless the fall didn't kill me, but only injured me, and *then* I burned alive.

Sometimes, I wish it were possible to just tell one's imagination to not go there. Or maybe I was the only person whose thoughts had morbid lives of their own on occasion.

I guess it couldn't be just me or horror movies wouldn't have audiences.

Climb!

Oya pushed me toward the tree. If I didn't do this on my own, she was going to take my limbs and force me. I'd prefer to try without her assistance.

I found a decent-sized branch and pulled myself up. That got me a foot off the ground. Blindly, I grasped for more. Smoke curled around me and made me cough.

Keep going.

You try this when you can't breathe. Now stop distracting me.

Surprisingly, that made her shut up.

Carefully, painfully, I continued to haul myself up the tree. Due to the smoke, I had no idea how far I was off the ground, which was the only silver lining to this misadventure.

I put my right hand down in the crook between two branches and something stung me. I pulled my hand back, expecting to see a small tongue of flame on the branch. Fuck my own stupidity; I'd been an idiot and put my hand in a live fire.

But the branch wasn't covered in flame. I blinked and wondered if I were hallucinating. Caught in the branch was a small sooty red feather. It was pretty, but not what I was here for.

Yes yes yes. Take it!

A feather? I'm here for a damn feather?

I grabbed it, not caring why it was important, only that taking it put me one step closer to getting Oya out of my head and me out of this damn inferno.

The feather stung my palm again, but this time I held on. And suddenly, I could breathe, and the heat, while still present, was not so unpleasant.

But there was something else. An awareness of what I needed to do next. I couldn't climb down the tree holding the feather in my hand, but I instinctively realized it wouldn't help me survive the fire if it weren't touching my skin. Awkwardly, I reached down and shoved it into my sock.

Getting down the tree was tricky; despite the fact I could now apparently breathe through the smoke, I couldn't see through it. Finally, I met the flames coming up and realized I had nothing else to do but jump and hope.

Any one of a thousand awful fates awaited me. I could spear myself on a branch that I couldn't see; I could land right in the middle of the fire; I could break a leg and be unable to escape. But what choice did I have?

I thought about Castro and held his image in my mind as I jumped. If this was to be my last thought, I wanted it to be of him.

I leaped.

The ground turned out to be about five feet down. Anticlimactic, but a welcome surprise.

Now, come get me.

I needed no more prompting. All it would take would be to follow the tugging in my mind to where Oya was. I staggered through the flames and the smoke, not heeding them at all, and only recoiling when they rose up in front of me and were not so easy to ignore.

I fought my way through the fire and hoped the feather stayed safely in my sock, because otherwise, I was in deep shit.

Shadows flitted around me, running back and forth in a panic. The shades of Cahokia were back. I must be getting close.

So close. Come!

And then there I was. At the small mound near which Mia and I had seen Pellagrio earlier in the day. The one Yama and Castro and I had walked past only a short while ago. Around it clustered hundreds of shades, and on top of it was a tall shadow with outstretched wings.

Oya. But from here, she looked as insubstantial as the others. She was trapped here, somehow, in between time, like a bug in amber.

For a moment, I was tempted to leave her here. I didn't want her to be free after what she'd done to Jordan, to me. She deserved to be trapped.

But then she'd never be out of my head.

One problem at a time. Get her out of my head, then figure out how to get her out of my life.

I pulled the feather out of my sock and held it out in front of me. I had no idea what to do, and Oya wasn't giving any directions. Perhaps she didn't know, either. After all, if she'd known what she was doing, she wouldn't have become trapped in the first place, right?

I walked up to the shadow figure, through the smaller shades, which did not notice me. When I got to it, I held out the feather and swiped it through the air.

Nothing.

In desperation, I shouted "abracadabra!" as I waved the feather around. I mean, why the hell not? What other plan did I have?

My right palm tingled. I stopped and tried to pay attention. Was the fire getting to me? Was Ware's mark helping me?

I knelt on the ground and pressed the mark to the spot where the winged creature's feet would be if she were solidly in our world. More tingling.

I put the feather on the ground, pressed my right hand on top of it, and closed my eyes.

Okay, bitch, this is it. This pulls you back or I'm leaving you here.

In my mind, I imagined a giant rope coming from my hand and attaching itself around the winged figure. I pulled on the rope.

Weirdly, since it was my imagination, you'd think the rope would be more cooperative. But it was hard to pull. Whatever I had caught in its loops was stuck hard and fast.

I tugged harder, and pulled with every ounce of willpower I had left. Slowly, I felt the invisible rope grow shorter. I was doing it! I continued pulling, despite my exhaustion, and the pain in my hand. It felt as if it were truly on fire now.

But I did not open my eyes. I had to finish this and escape the fire, get back to Castro and Petunia and my life. That my life now included crazy shit like this was something I tried very hard not to think of, not at this precise moment.

Right now, I just wanted to survive.

One final tug, and suddenly my imaginary rope dissolved. All at once, a physical presence popped into existence in front of me, and the grip Oya had on my mind melted away, but not pleasantly. More like something slimy wormed its way out of my mind and body. The feeling made me want to puke and took my balance away. I dropped to my knees, reeling internally.

"Finally," Oya growled. "Took you long enough. Now give me that feather."

13

I shook my head as I climbed shakily to my feet. "Nothing doing." It was the only thing standing between me and fiery death. I wasn't giving it up.

"You don't understand its power. It could destroy your world."

If Oya thought that was a good argument to make here, now, after what I'd been through in the past week, she was sorely mistaken. I laughed. "Oh, fuck, Oya, it seems to me any of you could destroy my world for any reason. What's a single feather got to do with it?"

I held the feather tightly in my right hand. Oya raised a hand to me, and I did the same.

"I need more power," she said. "I can't protect the Thunderer without help."

Leave it to one of these fucking creatures to stand in the middle of a fire and still only give partial answers.

"I don't know who or what that is, or why you think it's something you have to protect," I said. "Ware sent you for this, and you decided to use it yourself instead, and that fucked you up."

Her expression fell and she dropped her hand.

"I couldn't control it," she said simply. "But I have to learn, anyway. Ware will just store it away. I *need* it." She raised both fists this time, and stepped forward toward me. "Give it to me."

Yama appeared out of the flames. "Oya! I see the Lost found you. Stop tarrying; time to go. Mia needs you. Jordan, too." His tone was sharp, and the disapproval on his face needed no translation. He'd either figured out exactly what Oya and Mia had done to Jordan, or Mia had told him straight out. Either way, he was furious and not doing a terribly good job at hiding it.

"She has something of mine," said Oya. She didn't get any closer, but she didn't stop staring me down. "She will give it back."

"She has nothing that belongs to you," said Yama. "If what Ware sent you for is what I suspect it is, it's not even *his* to have. Now get to your lovers and your child and leave Teryl alone. This mess is a result of your own foolishness and pride. It has nothing to do with Teryl. Besides, what will Ware think if he knows what you did, and that you threatened Teryl?"

Oya visibly deflated, which was hard for someone of her height to do. It seemed that, even if she weren't afraid of me or Yama, she still had a healthy fear of Ware. Which made me think, once more, that I probably ought to be afraid of him, too.

"The fire departments have arrived," said Yama, "so follow me. I'll get you through the lines without any of us being seen."

He reached out and I gave him my left hand. In my right, I still clutched the feather. There was no way for me to let it go now without catching fire myself.

Yama pulled me through the fire. I did not see Oya. But eventually, we came out of the smoke behind the firefighters. The parking lot was crowded with fire trucks; our own vehicles weren't leaving the lot any time soon.

Castro, Mia, and Jordan waited near a crowd of onlookers who included the volunteers I'd seen at the Visitor's Center earlier. We ran up to them.

"Let's go," said Yama. "I've already sent for help and she's here." He gestured toward the main road.

We stumbled, following him to the road, where Lucy stood in front of a battered cargo van. Near her, the air was humid and heavy, a welcome relief from the hot dry air of the fire. I was reminded that Ware said she had power over water. Just what you wanted after running through flames. "Pile in," she said. "Let's get out of here."

Oya and Jordan helped Mia in first, but no one else touched her. Yama only shook his head. "Stupid," I heard him mutter under his breath.

The rest of us piled in after Mia was safely squared away. Mia clutched her locket and leaned against Oya. Jordan gazed at them both dazedly. Oya only had eyes for Mia. I wondered how the three of them were going to sort this out, but that was their own business. I leaned against Castro and welcomed his arm around my shoulders.

Lucy hopped in the driver's seat and got the van moving. Yama took shotgun.

As we crossed the river and got closer to the bar, Oya's attention moved to me. She stared at me and I knew she was just itching to get that feather back. It was clearly the item Ware had wanted her to procure for him.

Well, she wasn't having it. And neither was Ware. Not until I understood more. I didn't know how long that would take, but I was going to have to embrace this life now if I wanted to survive more than another week. I'd go back to my job, and learn what I could. I'd figure out if I had any abilities I could use against the Forlorn, and carve out my own place among them.

I'd tell Castro everything I'd learned, and we'd figure out how to get around, or through, these supernatural beings together.

The Arch passed by on our right. For the first time in my life, I felt, looking at it, like it was a source of stability and reason. I'd always imagined it reaching up to the sky, a monument to dreams. But now I saw it as a kind of fastener, pinning the city to the river and the ground. Holding on to the physical beauty of the world, and keeping it safe from those who would destroy it.

Nothing but imagination, but comforting nonetheless. Right now, I'd take comfort wherever I found it.

I nestled against Castro and tried to relax, but with Oya staring at me, it was difficult. I guess I'd made an enemy there.

Fine. She'd see what Teryl Gray was made of if she came for me. I twitched my right fist and her eyes locked in on the movement, then she met my gaze again.

I had no idea if she could still read my thoughts, but I nodded. *That's right, bitch. Come for me, and I'll hurt you.*

She switched her attention back to Mia. I kept my eyes on her.

No one spoke the rest of the way back to the Angels' Share. I had no idea how we were going to get home once we got there, but that was Ware's problem. I figured from now on, if I were another one of his special errand-runners, he'd be doing favors for me as well. A ride home for me and Castro was the least he could do.

Overhead, more thunder rumbled. Every time it did, Mia stirred uncomfortably. More crazy shit to worry about. But for now, I needed to put that aside.

Castro and I had a date with a funny movie, and damn it, we had a hedgehog waiting for us.

About the Author

 Marella Sands is a native St. Louisan who has published novels, short stories, and non-fiction works. Her historical novels, *Sky Knife* and *Serpent and Storm*, were set in 5th century Central America. *Sky Knife* has also appeared in a German edition as *Der Mayapriester*. In addition, she co-wrote two King's Quest novels with fellow St. Louisan Mark Sumner under the name Kenyon Morr. She has had short stories in several recent anthologies. She has always been interested in cemeteries, and sits on the board of one. She and her husband travel whenever they can and stop by old cemeteries when they have the opportunity.

Marella earned degrees in anthropology from the University of Tulsa and Kent State University. The author's household includes the author, her husband, and a multitude of pets.

Word Posse Fun Fact

This book took longer to get out than I wanted because I was busy writing other things that had actual deadlines. Tor was looking for some non-Western fantasy and I thought, why not? I composed a novella that is set in Thailand in the 19th century and is a sequel of sorts to the famous Thai ghost story of Mae Nak. Tor didn't buy it, but you can read it in Issue #85 of *The Grantville Gazette*. I was also invited into an anthology and that meant another interruption, but also a chance to write a story I've wanted to get to. Meanwhile, if you want to learn more about Mound 72, my favorite place at Cahokia Mounds State Historic Site in Collinsville, Illinois, check out its webpage at cahokiamounds.org/mound/mound-72/. Come by for a visit! Like Kutna Hora, which was mentioned in the last book's fun fact, Cahokia Mounds is a World Heritage Site.